THANK YOU FOR APPLYING

KRISTEN GRAFTON

COTTAGE HOUSE PUBLISHING

For my students,
past, present, and future:
I believe in you.

1

A mandated study hall for all seniors to have the opportunity to work on college applications seemed a little excessive to me, but that's the River Glen Academy way. Mrs. Champlain was supposed to be helping us as the librarian, but a lot of the seniors didn't really care and would rather be playing the Google Chrome dinosaur game instead of working. Besides, most college applications had been due back in November. At this point, the only colleges still accepting applications were on rolling admissions. We were mostly supposed to be working on either rolling admissions applications or scholarship applications, but I was one of the only students actually doing that. I didn't really get why some people didn't take college admissions seriously. I mean, this was possibly the most important decision of our lives. Choosing the right school was everything.

"Five more minutes," Mrs. Champlain shouted, and I started logging out of Google docs.

"Shoot," Wesley said from his seat next to me. "I only had a few more sentences to write on this essay."

"I told you not to put that essay off until today. Isn't it due tonight?"

"And it'll be done tonight."

"Your mom's going to kill you."

"Hey, I got my college apps turned in. That's what really matters. Those stupid things took forever."

"No kidding."

One of the worst things about applying to college was having to dig up all this old information that nobody knows about themselves. It starts simply enough: here, fill out this form with your full name—you know, the one you hate because it sounds like some southern grandma—then your address and every address where you've ever lived, then your parents' names and every address where they've ever lived, where they went to school (as if we college admissions readers care about that crap) and so on and so on. Then, for some reason, you have to prove your citizenship like a million times even though your family has lived in the same town for the last five generations. And don't worry if you don't know your social security number because you will by the twentieth time you have to type it in somewhere.

And then, assuming you've survived typing all of your personal information about your age, race, gender, extra-curriculars, grades, favorite books, blood type, surname origin—okay, maybe I'm exaggerating—then comes the joyous essay. And of course, no two colleges have the same essay prompts. One college wants to know about your favorite classic novel, another about discrimination you may have faced, another about what superpower you would choose, and yet another about which president you'd like to have dinner with. I'm not sure why colleges want to know about *To Kill A Mockingbird*, lack of funding for performing arts, my deep desire to fly, or Andrew Jackson, but here I am.

When the bell rang, Mrs. Champlain waved her arms erratically to get our attention.

"Mrs. Rush wanted me to remind you all that the scout from Florida State University is on campus today for the next hour. Any interested seniors are excused from their elective class today to go hear what FSU has to offer."

Matthew Altman raised his hand. "Can we skip math class instead? I'm failing, and I don't want a lecture from Mr. Davenport."

Mrs. Champlain frowned at Matthew, and I felt secondhand nervousness from the ire she directed at him. "Perhaps someone who is in danger of getting kicked off the wrestling team due to grades shouldn't be skipping College Algebra, don't you think Mr. Altman?"

Everyone laughed, and Matthew's wrestling teammates started slapping him on the back and high-fiving Mrs. Champlain. Mrs. Champlain always came in with the shade, I'd give her that.

Mrs. Champlain gave out additional information about FSU's visit, but I'd already tuned out. I wasn't skipping theater for a college visit from a school I had zero interest in. I already knew where I wanted to go.

"Are you going?" Wesley said, throwing his beat-up backpack over his shoulder. He'd had the same navy Jansport since freshman year and it really should've been replaced sophomore year, but he swore it was fine. I think the real story was he spent way too much money on it and he didn't want to admit defeat.

I shook my head. "I'd rather paint sets. You?"

Wesley twisted his mouth. "Don't think so. Can't picture myself living in Tallahassee."

Wesley and I parted ways with the other seniors outside of the library and headed for the cafeteria. It was almost laughable, actually, the idea that I would skip my favorite class of the day to hear from my least favorite Florida school. There was nothing wrong with FSU exactly, but it wasn't the perfect school.

Most people consider Disney World to be the main attraction in Florida, but as someone born and raised in the sunshine state—which is poorly named since it should have been called the insect state or the humidity state or something like that—let me be the one to set the record straight: The most magical place in Florida is not Disney World. In fact, Gainesville is home to the most magical place in Florida: The University of Florida.

What else does a kid who grew up in the middle of Florida have to dream about?

"FSU's not a terrible school, you know," Wesley said while we walked, "just because you hate it for no reason."

"Not for no reason."

Wesley gave me a skeptical look, and I couldn't help but laugh.

We slipped in the back door of the cafeteria so that we wouldn't have to walk through the main room where the floor gets really slippery when the janitors start mopping it at the end of the day. The cafeteria and the auditorium were one building and always had been. I guess it was too expensive to build a whole auditorium that would only get used for the semi-annual plays and for chapels and school assemblies, but it was a pain when we would have to rearrange all the chairs and stack the tables. At least it was a really nice stage.

Wesley and I dropped our bags off in the costume room and grabbed some paint and brushes from Mr. King.

"Ah, Mr. Dixon, Miss Haywood, I'm thrilled to see your commitment to the arts."

"Just here to finish painting the sets we started yesterday," I said

Mr. King thrust out a pair of paintbrushes and puffed his chest. "Well, when you paint, paint with passion. Paint with all of the passion that you will have when you perform knowing that the sets are imbued with the same enthusiasm, spurring you on to the most spectacular performance you can give—"

Wesley saluted him. "Will do, Mr. King. All the passion and all that."

We slipped away before Mr. King could go on because we both knew that if we let him, he'd never stop.

"He's so extra," Wesley said.

"Kind of makes sense for a drama teacher."

"Hey, did you finish the castle yesterday?" Wesley asked.

I shook my head. "We didn't have enough gray paint. I'll finish it now."

"Gosh, you're so slow." Wesley rolled his eyes and sighed. "I finished the jail cell forever ago."

"The jail cell is just one gray panel! Wait, is that where all the gray paint went?"

Wesley shrugged. "Maybe. I was completing a masterpiece."

"This," I pointed at the castle, "this is actual art."

"If you say so."

I crinkled my nose at him, and we both laughed. The entire theater class was supposed to be painting sets, but somehow it always ended up being just me, Wesley, Caroline, and Devon, and ever since Caroline and Devon got together, they had been completely useless. They would just stare at each other and giggle. It was nauseating.

I started working on the roof of the castle. When I found out that the musical this year was going to be *Beauty and the Beast*, I was so excited because I was convinced the sets were going to be beautiful. Then we found out the pre-made sets were too expensive and that we would have to make them. Somehow I didn't think I and my utter lack of artistic ability were up to the task. Caroline was actually the best artist in the class, but, well, you know.

"I just can't wear that. It makes me look so fat." The one and only Sienna West stormed onto the stage, knocking over the fireplace panel on her way.

"It does not," Rachel Graham said, holding Sienna's arm. "It just makes you look like a teapot."

"Maybe I don't want to look like a teapot."

Rachel furrowed her eyebrows in confusion. "But you're Mrs. Potts."

She scoffed. "You just don't get it."

Sienna stormed off as quickly as she stormed in, and Rachel followed her, trying to convince her that she would look beautiful dressed as a ceramic kettle.

Wesley snickered a little. "Guess she's still mad."

"You think?"

Sienna had played the lead role in every musical for the past two years, and she hadn't taken too kindly to being dethroned by Rachel. Not only was Rachel prettier, a better singer, a better actor, and basically the spitting image of Belle, but she was—*gasp*—a junior. Sienna screamed at Mr. King the day the cast list came out about how she should have some kind of senior privilege over Rachel, but Mr. King said something about Rachel possessing the aura of Belle or something, and that was that. Unfortunately for the rest of us, Sienna still whined every chance she got. She even prematurely dyed her hair brown because she was convinced she'd get the role, and even though she looked better as a brunette and she must've known it because it'd been brown ever since, that hadn't stopped her from reminding all of us of her "sacrifice" of dyeing her hair.

"Hey," Wesley said. "Maybe you should throw a fit like that, too. Maybe Mr. King will reconsider and give you a bigger role.

I laughed. "Not likely."

"You've got a better voice than Sienna."

"That's not much of a compliment."

"Still. Maybe if Sienna is successful in killing Rachel off and she gets Belle, you can be Mrs. Potts."

"I'll pass. I'm happy to be Bimbette #1 and stage director."

"If you say so."

"What about you? Why don't you pull a Sienna and try to get the role of the prince?"

"Too much pressure."

When Wesley got the role of Gaston, he was convinced it was a mistake. He swore it was because he was the only guy in theater tall enough and muscular enough to be convincing as Gaston without wearing an absurd muscle bodysuit. It was really because everyone knew Wesley was hilarious. Of course, it didn't hurt him that he was good-looking.

"So I heard back from UT last night," Wesley said suddenly without looking away from the set he was painting.

I whipped my head around. "And you're only just now telling me?"

Wesley cracked a smile. "I got in."

I threw my brush down in the can of paint and hugged him. The University of Tampa was Wesley's top choice, and even though the abbreviation sounded like an infection, it was a great school. He'd been sweating it ever since he submitted the application.

"That's fantastic. I knew you'd get in."

He laughed. "I didn't."

"Shut up, yes you did." I took a step back and squinted. "So that's the real reason you didn't want to go to the FSU meeting."

"Maybe." He shrugged. "Besides, I think you would actually burst into flames if I became a Seminole."

"No, *I* would burst into flames if I became a Seminole. So did you accept yet?"

"I've only heard back from two of the ten schools I applied to."

"So? UT is the one you wanted. The others were backups. Who cares now?"

"You're telling me that if you get into UF, you'll accept without considering any other option?"

"When I get into UF, that's exactly what I'll do."

"Not even USF?"

"Especially not USF."

"But those are the only two schools you applied to. Against my expert advice, mind you."

"I only applied to USF to make my mom stop talking about it. I'm going to UF. No question about it." There wasn't another option for me. If my mom had let me, I wouldn't have even applied to USF.

"Maybe I'll accept UT the day you accept UF. D-Day is still February 25th, right?"

"Yep."

"All right, February 25th it is then."

"Deal." Wesley and I shook hands.

2

Other than theater, government was probably my favorite class. As much as I loved AP English, government was taught by Ms. Corwin, the greatest social studies teacher known to man—or at least known to Polk County. The one consolation of being unable to take AP Government due to it being scheduled at the same time as Italian 3—thanks a lot to our administration for assuming no seniors would willingly take a third year of a language when it wasn't required—was that I got to have Ms. Corwin another year.

I took my usual seat—front left, by the window—and pulled out last night's homework. The bell had already rung, so class was quiet while Ms. Corwin took attendance, but I could just barely make out the sounds of Wesley *psst*ing me. I turned around, and he mimed a phone, so I slipped my phone out of my bag. Ms. Corwin was a real sweetheart, but she was the worst when it came to catching students on their phones. Most of the class blatantly texted in front of her. I tried not to do that because I liked her.

I opened the text from Wesley to read: *pencil to spare?* I rolled my eyes. Every day. I tossed him the pencil on my desk and grabbed another one from my bag. I slipped my phone under my leg just as Ms. Corwin came by.

"Happy Wednesday, everybody," Ms. Corwin said as she passed out some papers. "I'm very excited to tell you all about a wonderful opportunity you have as seniors." She smiled. It's worth noting that Ms. Corwin was really pretty. She was in like her late twenties or something like that. Another thing I'd always liked about her: she was young, which meant that she wasn't yet old enough to have forgotten what it was like to be in high school.

"The county is running a contest in the coming months for high school juniors and seniors. It is government-related, so I obtained permission to bring it to your attention as part of this class. As you can see from the handout, it is called 'Crossroads of Education and Government.' This is a new event that encourages students to get involved in politics. I think it sounds very interesting.

"Basically, it will operate like a science fair. You may enter independently or with a group of up to three people. Students will develop presentations on a topic of their choice that directly impacts them. These topics need not be political in nature, but they should be approached from a political perspective. In other words, why is this important to you and your peers? Why should your local, state, and maybe even national government take interest? What can be done to improve the circumstances surrounding your topic? Specifically, what issues directly impact your school and your education? And most importantly, what can you do as students to fix this problem?"

I kind of wished that this project had come earlier in the year. It actually sounded really interesting. This was right up my alley: student political involvement. But I didn't have time for it now.

Ms. Corwin continued: "These presentations are designed to be detailed and thorough. Judges will walk around and interview all students for about ten minutes each. You will need to have talking points ready, some kind of visual aid, possibly handouts, and direct and clear ways you want the local government to help. This project will be time-consuming and will require a lot of work." Several students in class groaned. "Here's the good news: this is not for a grade. I am not requiring you to enter this contest. However, before you shut your mind to it, let me offer a few incentives.

"First of all, Mr. Dale Henchard, owner of River Glen AutoMall is sponsoring the event. As a way of giving back to local schools, he is offering a charitable donation to the winning cause. As a more personal incentive, this contest comes with prize money for the winners. First place will receive $1000, second place $500, and third place $300. All three winners will be featured in the newspaper. Also, many college scouts will be attending the fair. Now, since the event will take place in April, all of your college decisions should be in by then. However, college scouts are prone to offering scholarships, removing students off of waitlists, or offering late admission based on events like these. If they like what they see, they will contact you, regardless of whether or not you win."

Huh. That was intriguing, I had to admit. I couldn't help but wonder if it would help me get a scholarship to UF. Still, I had a hard time imagining where in my schedule I was going to fit an elaborate project. Any time not committed to school or the musical would certainly be absorbed by my manager Gina who, if she found out I had any free time, would no doubt schedule me for extra shifts at Moe's.

"And finally, even though I am not requiring this, I will offer extra credit to any students who participate, and I would be more than happy to help you organize your projects. The extra credit will be substantial in proportion to the amount of work this project demands. Any questions about the basics?"

Rudy raised his hand. "So we don't have to do this, right?"

Ms. Corwin sighed. There was always one. "No, you don't, but at least consider it before you rule it out. Anyone else? No? Okay then. Please see me by the end of next week to tell me you are entering, and I will supply you with additional information. I will be submitting entry forms on your behalf. Now then, on to our class. Get together with the same partner you chose yesterday and finish those workbook pages about the Constitution. You've got twenty minutes to finish, and then we're moving on."

I moved to the back of the classroom and sat next to Wesley. Wesley always sat in the back. Said the front made him nervous. I always had to sit in the front to make sure I stayed focused. How could he possibly pay attention from back there? Maybe he didn't.

"All right, is number twenty-one the last one we did?"

"I think so," Wesley said, fidgeting with my pencil. "Hey, what do you think about that?"

"What?"

"The government thing Ms. Corwin was just talking about."

I shrugged. "Sounds interesting, I guess. I'll probably go and see all the different projects."

"You're not going to enter?"

"Wasn't planning on it. Why, are you?"

"I thought it seemed like a good idea. The money would be enough for me to finally fix up my car. Plus I need the extra credit."

I cackled. "You need the money for that beater, but you do *not* need the extra credit. You have like a 4.7 GPA or something."

"I need it if I'm going to beat out Ann for salutatorian."

Wesley and Ann had been neck-and-neck for salutatorian for the past two years, and since Riley was so far ahead of everyone else, making valedictorian basically impossible, the competition for salutatorian had been pretty intense. The only reason Wesley was behind Ann right now was that he kind of goofed off in AP Econ last semester and got a B+. He would probably still pass the exam, but Ann swamped him with an A.

"Well then enter. I'm not stopping you," I said.

"I was hoping you'd want to enter together. It would be easier if we worked together. Less work."

"I don't really feel like committing to all that right now."

"Why not? You could knock both me and Ann out of salutatorian contention."

"Yeah, right." I had long ago dropped out of contention for that. I was sixth in the class. I'd never catch Wesley or Ann because they both took AP Bio and I didn't. AP Chem was hard enough. I was being penalized for my hatred of science.

"Come on, it'll be fun. Plus, UF would probably be impressed."

"I'm not worried about UF being impressed."

"But you love politics. You want to major in political science."

"So?"

"Miss Haywood, did I just hear you say you're not entering the fair?" Ms. Corwin appeared suddenly behind Wesley. I'd never understood how she walked so quietly. "I was really hoping you would be interested in entering. You're one of my top students."

"I just don't think I have the time to devote to it. I've got a lot going on with school, work, the musical, and preparing for graduation."

Ms. Corwin nodded. "Fair enough. But please promise me that you'll reconsider. I think this is a really great opportunity for you to develop some skills that will help you in your chosen field. I know you plan on applying to UF's law school after college, and this is the kind of thing you could do now to show your commitment. You'll think about it?"

"I'll think about it," I said, though I knew I wasn't going to enter. I didn't need it. I probably would've done it last year, but now? I was too busy. And I knew UF would accept me without some kind of obvious pandering to college admissions boards.

***

"There is literally no way that the answer is 75," Rafael said to Drew. We'd only been in study hall for maybe twenty minutes, but those two spent the entire time arguing over their math homework. I was trying to work on my own math homework and tune them out, but their incessant arguing was making it difficult.

"How do you know it's not 75?" Drew asked, pointing his pencil accusingly at Rafael.

"Pretty sure our answer is supposed to have pi in it."

"Oh," Drew said quietly. "Well, you taught me wrong."

"Then don't sleep in class."

Drew put his head in his hands. "Ugh, I don't have time for math homework. I have a zillion lines to memorize."

"Zillion?" Wesley smirked. "We might've found the reason you're struggling with math homework."

Drew had gotten the big role: the Beast. He was ecstatic about it. He'd had a lot of lead roles over the years, but everyone knew he wanted to end senior year with a bang, and *Beauty and the Beast* gave him that bang.

Actually, I looked at the group I was sitting with—Wesley, Drew, Rafael, Devon, Caroline, and Jamar—and realized we were all in the musical. We'd all done the musical for years. Other than Wesley and I, none of us were really friends until we started doing the musicals together. Something about those long nights of rehearsals, delirious off-key singing at late practices, and inside jokes about on-stage mistakes that only we noticed bonded us all.

"At least your lines are normal," Rafael said. He was cast as Lumiere. "I don't know how I'm going to pull off a French accent."

"Dude, you did it in auditions," Devon said, barely glancing away from Caroline. "That's why you got the part."

"Yeah, an accent for six lines at an audition is one thing. It's going to be way harder to do it for a whole show."

Wesley held up a hand. "Why is Lumiere the only one with a French accent anyway? Isn't the whole thing set in France?"

I had always wondered that, too. I even suggested to Mr. King that we all do French accents to be authentic, but he brought up the pretty reasonable point that most of us couldn't do a believable French accent. At least we had talked him out of British accents for everyone except Lumiere. Why do people do that?

Jamar laughed. "Be glad you're not LeFou, Rafael. I have a whole song with rhyming adjectives about Gaston. It's really hard to keep them straight."

"I hope this thing turns out well," Rafael said, "because it's going to be a ton of work."

Drew added, "Right? Could you believe Ms. Corwin offering that extra credit project today? As if the seniors don't have enough to do already."

"Exactly," I said. "I love Ms. Corwin, but she kind of guilt-tripped me about not entering. I don't know where she thinks I'd find the time."

Wesley leaned in. "That's why I suggested teaming up. Less work."

"Still too much work." I went back to my calculus homework. I had to get this done. I had a shift at Moe's after school, and I did not want to have any homework to do when I got home.

"Shoot," Jamar said suddenly, bolting upright, "what time is it?"

Drew answered, "1:37."

"Crap, crap." Jamar whipped his laptop out of his bag and started typing furiously. "I completely forgot. Auburn's decision letters came out at one today."

We all waited quietly because we knew there was nothing we could say until he saw the decision. Auburn University wasn't Jamar's first choice—mostly because he was indecisive and didn't have a first choice—but it was high on his list. It's a good school. A lot of kids from River Glen had gone there over the years. I was actually a little surprised that no one else reached for their computers to check. I guess Jamar was the only one of us who'd applied there.

He clicked furiously and muttered a few hurried pleadings at his computer to move faster until he finally fist-pumped in the air and shouted, "Yes!" eliciting a shushing from Mrs. Champlain.

"You got in?" Wesley asked.

"Yeah, man," he answered, high-fiving everyone at the table. "Oh, that's a big relief. So far, I've only gotten rejections."

"Really? How many?"

"Only two out of the twelve I applied to, but I was starting to freak out."

"You applied to twelve schools?" Caroline asked. "That didn't seem excessive to you?"

"Not at all. I wanted to make sure I got in somewhere."

Wesley shrugged. "I mean, I applied to ten."

Rafael added, "Nine."

"Wow," Caroline said. "I applied to six, and I thought that was a lot."

"I wish there was one day that all application decisions came out," Wesley said. "I hate waiting for each individual school."

I said, "You already got into the one you wanted. Do the others matter?" I was only waiting on one letter. That's why I would have applied to only one school if my mom had let me.

"I guess not, but what if UT had been one of the last ones? I'd be stressing this whole time."

Jamar added, "I'm with you. At least now I've got one acceptance to fall back on."

"That's a really good fall back," Devon said. "Auburn's a great school."

"Yeah, they've got a really good physical therapy program. It's a contender for sure."

"Hey, did you guys hear Ann got into Vanderbilt?" Caroline said.

I couldn't help but raise an eyebrow at that. That's an incredible school. I wasn't surprised that Ann got in, but I knew she had her sights set on the Ivy Leagues.

"What day do UF and FSU come out?"

"The twenty-fifth," I said.

Wesley laughed. "Jorie's had that day marked on her calendar since freshman year."

"I'm really hoping I get into FSU," Caroline said. "That's my top choice."

"Me, too," Devon said. Of course they had the same top choice. They were probably planning to pick the same college. "I'm just so nervous. FSU's acceptances are so unpredictable."

"What do you mean?" Rafael asked. Rafael only moved to Florida a couple of years ago, so sometimes he didn't get our Florida references or associations. Every Florida native knew that the two big schools in the state were UF and Florida State University, or FSU. Florida had a lot of universities, but the UF vs. FSU rivalry was real, and both schools were popular choices for Florida high schoolers.

"They get so many applicants each year that you can never predict who will get in," Wesley explained to Rafael. "The test score requirements and GPA requirements change every year, and even if you have those scores, you're not guaranteed to get in because so many people apply. UF is the same way, which is why I told Jorie to apply to more than just UF."

Everyone's eyes focused on me, and I made a mental note to scold Wesley for that later.

Caroline said, "Jorie, you only applied to one school?"

I shrugged and tried to keep my eyes on my homework. "My mom wouldn't let me. I applied to two."

"Still, that's so risky. What if you don't get into either?"

I rolled my eyes. "That's not going to happen."

"It could."

"It won't."

"What's the big deal with UF and FSU, anyway?" Rafael asked, and several at our table gasped, eliciting laughter from all and another shush from Mrs. Champlain.

"Careful, man," Wesley said, "the Florida University Obsession Police will come for you if go around saying stuff like that."

"I've just never understood the obsession."

"UF and FSU are just the best schools in Florida," Caroline said. "I don't know. I guess it's just the way it is here. It's almost like a status symbol if you get into and go to one of them. Like, you're a successful Floridian and person."

"It's not like we have any of the Ivy Leagues in Florida," Devon added. "UF and FSU are our Ivys."

I laughed, but I kind of liked how Devon had put it. It was true. UF and FSU were Florida's Harvard and Yale in a weird way. You could choose not to go to UF and FSU. You could even choose not to apply to them, which would be weird but fine, but getting rejected by one or both of them? It was generally cause for embarrassment. It was failure.

Rafael turned to me. "So then what are you going to do if you don't get into UF?"

Why did everyone keep asking me that? "It won't be a problem. I'll get in. It's been my top choice for years, and I've done everything right. I know that I'll get in."

The more that people asked me that, the more annoyed I got because it made me start questioning myself. I knew UF's reputation for rejections. I knew that it was risky not to submit other applications. I knew that if I didn't get in after hyping it up so much that it would be really embarrassing. But I also knew that UF was the right school for me. I knew that I had done my research, gotten good grades, and varied my application as much as possible. I knew what I wanted to major in so I wouldn't be undecided. I had done extracurriculars and held a part-time job. I spent a lot of time on the application. I knew that I would get in because I had to. I had to go to UF, so I had to get in.

"I'll get in," I said again, mostly to myself.

3

— · —

One of my favorite things about taking AP classes was the freedom. Some people didn't see it that way since AP classes involved so much more work and deadlines and harsh grading, but that was exactly why I loved it; it weeded out the slackers. At least this way I didn't have to listen to Matt Altman ask why Mr. Darcy was so obsessed with Elizabeth Bennett since "all she does is read and what's hot about that?" I walked straight to the guidance counselor after that class and switched to AP.

We were supposed to be working on our essays on *Othello* right now, but UF's decision letters were scheduled to come out at 9:35, and I couldn't help but stare at the UF login screen and tap my laptop screen impatiently. Besides, I finished this essay two days ago—all I had to do was edit it.

I was refreshing the page over and over, waiting for it to hit 9:35, when Taylor swatted my arm. "Stop tapping," she said. "It's really annoying."

Mrs. Tipton had never really cared if we talked in class as long as we were still working, so she didn't even notice Taylor talking or me jumping three feet in the air because she startled me.

"Does it seem like this class is taking forever to you?" I said.

"No, but I didn't apply to UF. Besides, I thought you were going to wait until after school to check."

"Wesley suggested that. That doesn't mean I agreed."

"But what if you—"

"Don't finish that sentence."

"But it could happen. UF gets so many applications that really good students get rejected all the time. It would just be really awkward if—'

"Taylor." It does happen every year. So many qualified applicants not enough spots. But that won't be me. It *can't* be me.

Taylor raised her hands in surrender. "Fine, fine. Have you finished the essay yet?"

"Yeah, days ago," I said without looking in her direction.

"Well, will you proofread mine later? You know, when you're not burning your eyes out obsessively staring at a screen?"

"Sure."

Taylor set a copy of her essay on my desk, and I slipped it into my backpack without even looking. Other than Wesley, Taylor was probably my closest friend. We'd known each other since we were five since we had both gone to River Glen since kindergarten. The day I saw her throw a block at David Fletcher because he said "girls can't play with blocks" was the day I knew I wanted to be best friends with her. We hadn't always taken the same classes throughout high school, so it'd been harder to stay close, but I had managed to convince her to take AP Lit since she spent literally all of her time reading, and I was so glad I did. This was the only class we had together.

9:34. This was it. In exactly one minute, my future started.

The really fantastic thing about getting this decision during school was that Sienna was in this class. She'd been bragging since freshman year about how she'd have her pick of schools because she'd led such a "unique life" as she put it. We all knew that was code for: "my Daddy is rich and pays a lot of money to alumni associations to make sure I get in." Not that she wasn't smart, but you know, money talks. Getting that acceptance letter right in front of her would feel incredible, especially if somehow the bribes didn't work and she didn't get in.

I ended up daydreaming about the look on Sienna's face when I got in and she didn't, so I totally missed when the clock switched to 9:35. I logged in as quickly as I could, mistyping my password only once, and started clicking furiously to get to the right page. Every year, UF's server would crash because of all the high schoolers checking their admissions decisions, so I wanted to get in before that happened.

I finally got to the last click. I hesitated just the slightest bit before clicking the button that said "click here for your admissions decision." UF uploaded the letter itself that they mailed to your house later, so you had to scroll a bit to get past all the addresses and crap. Didn't they understand that we needed an immediate decision?

I scrolled past all the header information and started scanning for that one word that matters: congratulations. When I saw the line that read, "Dear Miss Marjorie Haywood," I hesitated for the slightest bit once again before scrolling.

There used to be an unspoken rule about college admissions. If the envelope was skinny, you didn't get in, and if it was fat, you did. In the computer age, the rule is this: If the first word is "Congratulations," you got in. If the first words are "Thank you for applying," you didn't. So when I scrolled past my name and saw the words "Thank you," my heart and my stomach decided to switch places in my body. I suddenly felt incredibly nauseated. My hazy brain pieced together the words "Thank you for applying to the University of Florida. However, due to a large volume of applicants..." It was there that I stopped reading as a form of self-preservation. I didn't need to know what the rest of the letter said. Just useless condolences that were meant to give the illusion that I wasn't a total failure.

"Yes!" Sienna jumped out of her seat and nearly knocked her thousand dollar laptop on the floor. "I got in. I got into UF."

Her friends cheered for her, like lemmings, and she soaked it all up. I was vaguely aware that Taylor was talking to me, asking me something, but I couldn't help but stare at Sienna, her perfect hair bouncing just perfectly, her already too short skirt getting just a little shorter with each jump. It was a wonder, really, that she hadn't gotten written up for her skirt being that short. Weren't uniform skirts all supposed to be the same length? And why did snobby rich girls like that always wear such loud bangle bracelets? It's like they needed everyone to be aware of their existence at all times.

"Jorie, are you okay?" Taylor whispered.

I opened my mouth to respond, but Sienna interrupted. "So, Jorie, did you get in? Maybe we'll be classmates again. That would be cool, wouldn't it? I mean, that's if we have classes together. I don't know how much we'd actually see each other." She waited for a response, but I didn't give her one. "So? Did you get in?"

The worst thing about girls like Sienna was that they seemed perfectly nice. People always believed that they were nice because they sugarcoated everything. Like the southern equivalent of "bless your heart." You could be as insulting as you wanted as long as you gave the illusion of being nice.

"Of course I got in," I said before I could stop myself. "But you're right, I don't know how much we'll talk in college since I'll be a little busy. What are you majoring in again? Have you even decided?" I threw in a smile to soften the dig I just gave her.

"Okay, okay," Mrs. Tipton said. "Congratulations to those who got into UF. It's a great school and a great option. Now let's get back to those essays. But first, would anyone be willing to run an errand for me?"

My hand shot up. "I will." I needed to be out of this room. I didn't even care what the errand was.

"Thank you, Miss Haywood." Mrs. Tipton wrote a pass and handed me a stack of papers. "Would you run these over to Mr. Bronson's office?"

I took the papers, the pass, and rushed out of the door as quickly as I could without looking like I was rushing. Mr. Bronson's office was just down the hallway, but I chose to take the long way back after I dropped off the papers to avoid going back to class. In the little garden tucked behind the main building, I sat down on a bench, holding my head in my hands.

How could I have not gotten into UF? I had a 4.5 GPA, I'd taken six AP classes, I was in four honor societies, I had volunteered in childcare at my church for the last five years, I'd been in the last seven musicals, I was on the swim team for two years, I'd had a part-time job for two years, I got a 1300 on the SAT, and four of my teachers wrote beautiful recommendation letters. I was the perfect candidate for UF.

I immediately started running through all the things in my head that could have possibly hurt me. Maybe it was because I wrote my essay about President Jackson. I don't idolize the guy or anything, but I thought he was interesting. Maybe it seemed like I endorsed him. Maybe he was too controversial of a president to write about. But wasn't that the point? I thought a controversial topic would be eye-catching, but maybe it was just a nail in the coffin. Maybe I went too far and should have played it safe.

Or maybe it was because I went to a private school. Did it look like I was trying to hard or that I was some snob who thought I was better than everyone else? Or maybe it was because I lived in the middle of nowhere. Who had even heard of River Glen, Florida, anyway?

Or maybe I should have applied for early admissions, even though they claim that doesn't make a difference. Or maybe I shouldn't have applied to live on campus. Maybe I shouldn't have put political science as my major. Maybe I submitted my application too early, and I should have worked on it longer.

Or maybe I just wasn't good enough. Maybe UF hated me the second they saw my application. Maybe I was not UF material. What was I supposed to do if that was the case? I'd been convinced that UF was the right choice for me for years. I'd told everyone I was going there. I'd been bragging about getting in for months. What would I tell everyone?

And where would I go now?

4

—·—

The rest of the school day was a daze. I avoided Wesley as much as I possibly could so that we wouldn't have to talk about *it*. During study hall, I asked to go to the library so that I could be away from Sienna and Wesley and Taylor and all of them. I even asked Mr. Stevens if I could leave a few minutes early so that I could get to my truck and leave before Wesley made it to the parking lot. Since we always parked next to each other and we both had last period free for work release, I had to get away as quickly as possible.

I worked my usual shift at Moe's, but I was on autopilot the entire time. All I wanted was to go home, planning to drown my sorrows in my mom's marshmallow fudge brownies, but the second I walked through the door, I knew that I wouldn't be granted the isolation I wanted.

You know how you can just tell that your parents know something and they want you to know but they don't want to tell you? It's like this excitement and energy is pouring out of them like a waterfall but they act weirdly when you ask them why they're acting weirdly.

At first, I didn't know why they were acting like that, and I really didn't have the patience to deal with whatever weird thing they were in the middle of. I desperately wanted to ignore them, but when I realized that they were standing by the endless stack of mail, I knew what was going on.

"Hello, sweetie," my mom said with a smile too wide for her face. "How was school?"

"Fine."

"Did you get a lot done with the pictures today?" My dad knew nothing about theater, but he was supportive nonetheless.

"The sets, Dad. And yes. The castle is pretty much done now."

"That's great, honey." Smiles. Smiles all around.

"Well I have a lot of homework to do." I tried to dart past them to my room, but my mom took hold of my arm.

"Wait, you just got home."

"So?"

"But we want to talk."

"Why?"

"We have to have a reason to want to talk to our beautiful, intelligent daughter?"

"Oh my gosh, make it stop," my sister Savannah shouted from the couch. "The letter's on the table."

I glanced down at the envelope to see the USF letterhead. Figures. My mom was obsessed with the University of South Florida. She'd been saying that was the school for me since I was in middle school. She claimed it had nothing to do with the fact that USF was a little less than an hour away, but let's be real.

Of course there was nothing really wrong with USF. It seemed like a great school—for somebody, anyway. Savannah would probably go there. She wanted to study medicine, and USF seemed like a fine place to do that. But not me. I wanted to get out of this place, away from home, on my own. I only applied to USF to make Mom happy and as a back-up. River Glen made us all pick back-ups. Mine was USF.

Besides, if I was going to law school at UF—and I *was* going to law school at UF—then I couldn't get my pre-law political science degree from a school that wasn't known for it. How would that look?

Of course now, everything was in jeopardy. UF didn't want me. Maybe their law school wouldn't either. Maybe I was destined to stay stuck in this place, this tiny map-dot town with nothing to do and nowhere to go. Maybe the only hope I had of escape or progress was *Tampa* of all places. My mom would get her way then. What a depressing thought.

I couldn't even decide if not getting into USF either would have been worse than getting in. Maybe going to a community college on my own terms would be better than going to the school my mom picked out for me, like I was in preschool or something.

And I definitely didn't want to see a letter, acceptance or not, without a UF letterhead.

My parents' faces looked like they might explode from anticipation, so I opened the letter. It was a thick envelope, which was usually a good thing. USF actually already uploaded my admissions decision on their application website, but I never bothered to check. If my parents knew the password—heck, if they even knew that the letter was uploaded—they probably would have checked themselves. This paper letter was just a courtesy.

I tossed the envelope aside and unfolded the letter. It was long and wordy, but I saw the one word that mattered: Congratulations.

My mother squealed almost at a dogs-only decibel, and my dad did this weird "woo-hoo" cheer-dance combo, and normally I might've laughed, but seeing their excitement made me want to scream.

"She did it," my mom squealed. "Can you believe it? She got into USF."

Dad added, "I always knew she could. USF would be stupid not to admit her."

Well, UF definitely wasn't stupid, so there must have been something wrong with me.

"Savannah, aren't you proud of your sister?" my mom asked my sister who wasn't even paying attention.

"Yeah, sure."

"I've got the most fantastic idea," Mom said, suddenly gripping her very startled husband's arm. "We should plan a visit to USF."

"Why?" I asked, trying to suppress the irritation in my voice.

"To see the campus, silly. It's beautiful. When I was there for that conference, it absolutely blew me away." A couple of years ago, my mom went to this conference at USF with the insurance firm she worked for and she'd been even more obsessed with USF ever since. She'd actually tried to get me to go on a campus visit months ago, but I had managed to get out of it at the time by complaining about having too much work to do while also filling out college applications. I had hoped that if I delayed it long enough, she would drop it, but apparently my mother was more stubborn than I had planned for.

"But what's the point? I already know that I don't want to go there."

"It's good to consider your options, Marjorie," Dad said. "USF is a good school. It wouldn't hurt to swing by and take a look."

"Road trip!" Savannah shouted, pumping a fist in the air.

"But I don't want to go there," I said again, more insistent this time.

"You haven't even looked at it, really. Maybe once you see it, you'll feel differently. I know you've got your heart set on UF, but you haven't heard back yet, and even if you do get in, USF is still worth considering." She put her arm around my shoulder. "With a school as big as UF, there are no guarantees about admission, and it wouldn't hurt to keep your mind open—"

"Enough with USF already." I threw my mother's arm off my shoulder. "I know you think it's the holy grail of colleges, but I don't want to go there. And I don't want to spend hours walking around a campus that I'll never step foot on again."

My parents tried to say something in response, but I muttered something about writing a paper, and they reluctantly let me go.

Closing the door behind me, I flopped onto my bed on my stomach, flipped open my laptop, and pulled up *Gilmore Girls* on Netflix. I'd watched every episode at least one hundred times, but it was my comfort show that I would put on in the background when I was doing homework or when I needed something to cheer me up. And this was certainly a day that I needed to be cheered. I chose to watch an episode from when Rory quit Yale, because honestly, if Rory can be stupid and drop out of school for literally no reason, then me not getting into UF couldn't be that bad, right?

Unfortunately, I barely made it past the theme song before Savannah burst into my room. Fortunately, she knew better than to enter my room uninvited without bringing me a brownie. She tossed the paper bowl with the delicious fudgey block onto the corner of my bed, and I took it without acknowledgment. Instead of leaving, she sat down on the edge of my bed and munched on her own brownie.

"Care to knock?"

"Nah, I'm good," Savannah said around a mouthful of brownie. "What's with you?"

"What?"

"You're in a mood," Savannah said.

"Maybe that's because you're getting brownie crumbs on my bed."

"You're eating brownies on your bed, too."

"I'm not in a mood."

"'She said moodily.'"

I glared at Savannah and she shut my laptop, so the last thing I heard was Logan's annoying voice. I'd always be team Jess.

"Why don't you just admit it?"

"Admit what?" I said.

"That you didn't get in to UF."

"Why would you say that?"

"Because I know that the UF decisions went out today, and if you had gotten in, you would have waltzed into the house and gloated, not snapped Mom's and Dad's heads off. And you know it."

I collapsed back against my headboard and clutched my dolphin pillow from Sea World against my chest. Sisters are so annoying because they know everything about you and they flaunt it.

Reluctantly, I looked up at Savannah, but she was almost expressionless, sitting up straight but not rigid. I expected another snarky response or gloating or even an "I-told-you-so" since she warned me over and over about applying to more schools, but nothing. She just looked at me.

"So why didn't you get in?"

"You think I know?"

"Don't they tell you when you get the letter?"

"That's not how admissions letters work," I said.

"Surely it says *something*."

Savannah grabbed my laptop and typed furiously. I used to change my password practically once a week because Savannah would always figure it out, but I gave up long ago. What was she going to find other than my term papers and Netflix?

Part of me wanted to stop her from finding the email, but part of me was just too exhausted to care. So what if she read it? It wouldn't change anything. She'd see for herself that it was hopeless.

"You should really clean out your inbox," she said.

"I don't like deleting things."

"It's cluttered."

"You get, like, infinite space with Gmail."

"Whatever. I found it. 'Dear Miss Marjorie Haywood—'"

I threw the dolphin at her. "Don't read it out loud."

"Too late. 'Dear Miss Marjorie Haywood, Thank you for applying to the University of Florida. Unfortunately, due to a large volume of applicants, the admissions committee has offered admission to the maximum number of candidates and is therefore unable to make a final decision regarding your application. However, because of your outstanding achievements and excellent application, the committee has voted to place your name on a waiting list.'"

I sat up. "A waiting list?"

"'The number of applicants granted admission from the waiting list varies year to year. Should a spot become available, we will notify you immediately.' Jorie, this is great."

"How is this great?"

"You didn't get rejected, you're just on a waiting list. You could still get in."

I slumped back again. "It's not likely." Just because she was the optimistic one didn't mean she knew any better. "People don't get off waitlists once they're on them. It's like a cheater way to reject someone. UF is just taking a cop out of actually telling me they don't want me."

Savannah crinkled her nose and continued reading. "'Should anything about your application or academic status change in the coming weeks, please notify us immediately as that may impact your place on the waiting list. Again, thank you for applying. Please contact us with any questions or concerns you may have.' Well, there you have it."

"What?"

"Just do something to change your status."

"Like what?"

"I don't know, something impressive. Cure cancer or something."

"Oh yeah, I'll just get right on that in between second and third period."

Savannah shrugged. "Worth a try, isn't it?"

I waved my hand at Savannah. "Shoo. I have to do homework."

"Psh. You're just going back to *Gilmore Girls*."

Savannah left, and I twisted my mouth at how well she knew me. I fired up Netflix again and hauled my backpack onto my bed to start doing homework. I had a ton of calculus homework to do, and the more I put it off, the worse it would get. But when I reached for my calculus textbook, I found my government homework stuck to the tape on the outside. One of the crunched up papers was the government project Ms. Corwin had been pushing. I casually skimmed the assignment and remembered how much work this sounded like—design an entire project to make local representatives care about some random issue?—but then I remembered something Ms. Corwin said: college scouts came to these kinds of things. This might be my way off the waiting list at UF. And that made any assignment worth it.

But I had to be sure. So I grabbed my computer and fired off an email to UF Admissions with a link to the event's website. I even included a short plea that I hoped didn't sound cloying asking if this would make a difference in my standing. I felt nervous about sending it. What if it made me look desperate or infantile? But I had to know. I *had* to. I needed a chance, and maybe this was it.

5

—·—

"Still want a partner?" I said to Wesley the next morning practically as soon as I'd gotten out of my truck and waved goodbye to Savannah.

"For what?" he said.

"The government project." I grabbed my River Glen cardigan and switched it out for my non-school-approved Adidas hoodie. Even though it felt ridiculous to wear a sweater outside in Florida, I always froze in the classrooms.

Wesley squinted. "I thought you didn't have time for that."

I shrugged, and we started walking toward the main building. "I changed my mind."

"Why?"

I didn't want to tell Wesley that I didn't get into UF. I *couldn't* tell him. I couldn't tell *anyone* because then they would know that I wasn't good enough. "It will look good since I want to major in political science."

"*I'm* the one who told you that."

I glared at him. "Do you want a partner or not?"

He smiled wide. It was hard to be mad at Wesley when he smiled that goofy, cheesy smile. It was also hard not to think about how I was lying to his face. "You've got a deal. Now we just need a topic."

"I'm sure we can come up with something incredible."

"Hey, I don't need incredible. I just need good-enough-to-get-extra-credit. And maybe win some money."

"Well I need incredible."

"Why?"

I forced myself to smile. "I'm hoping it'll help me get a scholarship to UF."

"So you got in? Congrats!" He gave me a big hug, and I forced myself to at least appear calm. In reality, I felt like screaming or running away or crawling into a hole to die, but I refused to let Wesley know any of that, as hard as it was to look him in the eye and lie to him. He was assuming—*everyone* was assuming—that I was a shoe-in for UF. How could I admit that I had failed? "So did you not get financial aid or something?"

I bit my lip. "I don't know yet, but it can't hurt to shoot for a scholarship."

"By the way, what happened to you yesterday? You disappeared."

I tried to shrug casually. "I picked up an early shift at work." It was the only thing I could think to say that would sound even quasi normal.

"The Mexican food business never sleeps, eh?"

I laughed. "Not at Moe's it doesn't."

"By the way, why are you here so early? You're not one of the cursed few with teachers for parents. You could sleep in."

"You didn't see the email, did you?" Wesley shook his head, and I rolled my eyes. Wesley was terrible about checking his email. In tenth grade, he first read an email from our ninth grade history teacher about a homework assignment he had forgotten to turn in. "Mr. King wants to have a meeting about the play."

"Did he say why?"

I shrugged. "Probably something about costumes. Remember, he was waiting to hear back from that consignment shop about pricing."

We headed to the back of campus to the cafeteria. Mr. King could've had meetings in a classroom—he did have one after all—but he always wanted to meet on the stage. He claimed it helped us keep in character, even when we weren't acting.

"Yeah, but what kind of costumes are those gonna be? Gaston will end up being '70s Saturday Night Fever style."

"Or worse—Romeo and Juliet with those classic shirt frills."

We laughed on the way in, but once we hit those blue tile floors in the cafeteria, it was like the room dictated the mood. Everyone was quiet, Mr. King was sitting at the piano plunking keys absent-mindedly, and nobody seemed willing to say the first word.

"Mr. King?" I said.

"Yes, Miss Haywood?" he said without looking up.

"I think everyone's here."

"Hmm?"

"For the meeting? Sarah walked in behind us, and I think she was the last one. We could probably start now."

I wish I could've said that this was a rare occurrence, but Mr. King was always like this. It was like he was up in the clouds and had to be forcibly dragged back down to earth as if earth was a disappointment. Today, the expression on his face convinced me that it was.

Mr. King stood up from the piano but did not leave its side, seeming afraid to leave its safety. "When I was young, I used to think that the worst thing that could happen to an actor was to be booed off of a stage. After years of struggling to get a decent role, I decided the worst thing was not to be on a stage at all. It seemed to me that teaching drama would guarantee that I would always be in close proximity of a stage. It appears I was wrong once again."

Everybody looked around at each other. It seemed no one quite knew what to say. For once, Sienna's forcefulness proved useful when she asked, "What does that mean, Mr. King? What are you saying?"

"By now I'm sure you've all heard the tragic news about the closing of Bill's Burger Bonanza."

Everyone exchanged awkward glances. Bill's Burger Bonanza was a local restaurant that had gone out of business a few weeks earlier. It was a decent restaurant—and the burgers were definitely good—but this was hardly front page news. Unfortunately, a lot of businesses had been going under. Times were tough, and a lot of small, local businesses just couldn't hack it. Most of us had become kind of numb to the closures. It seemed like there was at least one per month. It didn't really seem relevant to *Beauty and the Beast*.

Sienna folded her arms. "Who cares?"

"*Who cares?*" Mr. King put a hand to his chest as if he were having a heart attack while performing a scene from *Hamlet*. "Miss West, we should all care when one of our friends has to give up on their dream. As performers who seek to understand the human psyche and communicate the complexity of human emotion, we should be wrought with grief to our very souls at the sight of suffering. We should be crushed, devastated, and broken for those dreams deferred. We should—"

"It's just a fast food joint," Sienna huffed.

Mr. King pinched the bridge of his nose and sighed. "It is a travesty. Not only has our little town lost a wonderful eatery with the most spectacular sweet potato fries you've ever seen, and not only has a friend lost his life's work, but we, the thespians of River Glen Academy, have lost our biggest sponsor."

Everyone started whispering, and the whispers grew louder until Mr. King silenced everyone with a choir conductor's cue.

"Will that impact our production?" I asked. I knew the budget for the musical had taken a bigger hit than usual this year. These productions were funded pretty much entirely by ticket sales and sponsors. One of our other sponsors had already pulled out because they similarly couldn't donate substantial money and still expect to keep their business afloat, and Mr. King had struggled to get parents to donate even though many of them had the means to do so, but we were already doing so much of it ourselves. Would this really matter that much?

"Bill Bunton and I had discussed his financial concerns earlier this year. He had significant reservations about being able to donate this time. He felt that he would know better in the new year. He tried to convince me to cancel the musical back then, and maybe I should have, but I held out hope that either he would pull through or one of our other lovely patrons of the arts would be able and willing to save the production, but alas, no one has stepped up at this time. And for that reason, I must with the heaviest of heavy hearts announce that the musical will not be going forward."

There was an immediate uproar as the realization hit all of us. Sienna's voice hit a disturbing decibel as she shrieked about how everyone was out to get her; several of the musicians complained about having to learn so much music already; Drew, the Beast, sadly admitted that he'd planned to use this performance as an audition tape; and several of the underclassmen started asking about next year and whether the future of the department was in jeopardy as well.

Wesley and I exchanged a glance that seemed to say everything at once. We both really enjoyed the musicals every year. I'd been in the productions since eighth grade, Wesley since fifth, and we were both really looking forward to our senior year production.

I remembered over the summer when Wesley and I speculated about what musical Mr. King would choose. We both hoped it would be something fun that would actually turn out well. We even joked about how maybe Mr. King would pick a musical with a male-heavy cast like *Newsies* or something just to spite Sienna. *Beauty and the Beast* seemed like the perfect choice, and when Rachel was cast, even better. We both had roles that we liked, and Mr. King had some really great ideas for the choreography, but we'd barely gotten anywhere before it all got shut down.

I stood up, and even though everyone around me was still talking, I made eye contact with Mr. King and said, "But we've already made some of the sets. We have our own stage and lighting. How much more money could we possibly need?"

"Quite a bit. I can no longer afford to hire the guy who usually manages our sound and lighting, our sets have yet to be finished, costumes are going to cost a fortune, and we can't produce the playbills or film and record the performances if we can't afford the rates, and since selling those is a big money-maker, I'm not sure what else I can do. Do you all remember that we had to replace the microphones last year because most of them had broken? We had to eat into this year's budget to do that, so we're running a deficit as it is. Besides, Bill isn't the first sponsor we've lost, just the biggest. We lost a few others as well for financial reasons."

"And there's nothing else the school can do?"

Mr. King shook his head. "The budget's been straining as it is."

"What about next year?" Rachel asked. "Will we be able to do a musical next year? Could we find new sponsors?"

Mr. King nodded. "I'm hopeful, Miss Graham, but nothing is set in stone or written in the stars, I'm afraid. I simply can't get the money we need together this quickly, but maybe if I had more time—"

"Well that doesn't exactly help me, now does it, Rachel?" Sienna glared, and for a moment, I had the horrifying yet somewhat hilarious thought that she might slap Rachel across the face. "The *seniors* in this production deserve to have their moment in the spotlight."

"If I knew of any other way, Miss West, I would traverse the road not taken to bring this production to life, but I have no other options. Regretfully, this will be the last cast meeting for *Beauty and the Beast*. Our illustrious principal would like us to take down the sets by next week."

"Of course," Sienna said, "because Mr. Quentin has never cared about the arts. Why should he start now?"

Mr. King tried to argue, but Sienna had already stormed off the stage. In her absence, everyone else talked a little more freely as they picked up their bags and prepared to head out. I saw at least three people crying. I wasn't exactly the crying type, but this one stung. If Mr. King had in fact cut the musical earlier as Bill Bunton had urged him to do, it might have hurt less. People wouldn't have been cast, gotten excited, started painting plywood. Now it wasn't just something that was unreal—it was something that had been lost.

I walked over to Rachel and smiled. "Ignore Sienna. She's not mad at you. She just needs someone to take out her frustration on."

Rachel forced a smile. "I know. I don't blame her for being upset. I was really looking forward to this one. I've never been a lead before."

"And you would have been phenomenal."

She shrugged. "Maybe next year. I wonder if it'll be *Beauty and the Beast* again or if Mr. King will pick something different." She looked around to see if anyone was listening to us. "It might sound silly, but I was looking forward to wearing that gold dress, whatever it might have looked like."

"Hopefully it wouldn't have been an '80s catastrophe."

"Even then," Rachel laughed. "Plus, getting to kiss Drew wouldn't have been the worst thing."

"Wait, that's *not* why you tried out for the role of Belle? I assumed that was everyone's motivation for trying out for Belle."

She smiled. "That was just a fringe benefit, but no. I don't know, I've never really been good at anything else. I do okay in school, but I'm not like you, and I don't play any sports or draw or anything like that. I guess this is the one thing I'm really good at." After a pause, she added, "I hope that doesn't sound arrogant."

I shook my head. "Not at all. Theater has never exactly been what I'm fantastic at, but it's my favorite part of the year every year. I'm really disappointed it won't be happening. I hope you get to do it for your senior year."

"Me, too."

Rachel waved as she walked away, and I felt for her. Rachel would have another chance to be a lead next year, but she wouldn't have another chance to be Belle. For some of the underclassmen, this was supposed to be their first production. Plus, all of the seniors were missing their last chance. What I had said to Rachel was true: I wasn't the best actor or singer, but I really enjoyed the musicals. Not being able to do my senior year production was really upsetting. Looking at Wesley's face, I could see he was pretty devastated, too. Some of the students were handling it better than others, but everyone looked incredibly disappointed.

This was the kind of thing that happened in high school. Everyone acted like high schoolers have all this freedom or ability to choose for themselves, but they never really understood how much of a high schooler's life was dictated by outside forces. It always seemed like, once people weren't in high school anymore, they completely forgot what it was like to be there, to be that age, to know what it was like.

Sure, I'd had the freedom to pick theater over sports, but what did it matter if the option were taken away?

When you're young, everyone tells you not to underestimate your abilities, that you can do or be anything you want. Right now, I wished that were true. I really wished there were a way that I could save the musical.

***

"That's a stupid idea," I said.

Wesley and I had been brainstorming for the entire lunch period, but so far, we'd been unsuccessful, and it felt like the ideas were getting sillier.

"How is that a stupid idea?" Wesley wrinkled his forehead.

"No one would pay money to go to a cattle fair."

Wesley pointed at me and squinted. "People pay money for that all the time and you know it. Isn't that the whole purpose of county and state fairs? The Strawberry Festival does it every year."

"That's different. It's professional. No one wants to see the cows of high school students who are barely passing Ag." Agriculture classes—usually known as "Ag"—were definitely a big part of life in middle-of-nowhere-Florida, but I'd never understood the purpose. The kids who were actually really good at raising cattle were good because their families were cattle ranchers; they didn't need Ag class.

"Well then *you* come up with an idea."

I scrunched my face and bit the end of my pencil.

"Not so easy, is it?"

"It's not that. I just can't stop thinking about the musical."

Wesley's face dropped a little. He hadn't admitted it to me yet, but I knew he was disappointed. He liked the musicals a lot more than he would ever let on. I knew he was really looking forward to being Gaston. Last week, I caught him practicing one of his solos in his car in the school parking lot before school. He must've turned three shades of red when he realized I had caught him. "Yeah, it's lame, but what can you do?"

"There's got to be *something* we can do."

"You make enough money at Moe's to fund an entire high quality musical?"

"I don't make enough to fund a low quality musical. But there's got to be another way. Maybe we can do some fundraising or something."

"I doubt we could get enough money fast enough. Bake sales make, like, $300 at best. We need thousands."

I tossed my pencil down on the table and tried in vain to brush my hair back as the wind continued to throw it into my face. Normally, Wesley and I avoided eating lunch in the courtyard behind the gym because the Florida heat made it unbearable except in January, but we needed some peace and quiet to work on our government project. We still didn't have an idea, and we needed to move fast.

"We've got to focus on this stupid project."

"Look," Wesley said, spreading his hands out, "it doesn't need to be spectacular or anything. We don't need to solve world hunger or something. We just need something that's creative enough."

"No, it needs to be really good. I want to win."

"I do, too. I mean, I'd love to be able to fix up my car. I feel like that entire thing is going to fall to pieces one day like a bad cartoon. But it's senior year. We can come up with something that won't require too much time or work."

"'Cause that sounds like a winning idea. 'Here's our presentation, it didn't take too much time or work.' How is that going to win?"

"What's with you today? Are you stressed about UF?" he asked, and immediately I felt panic rising in my chest. I still hadn't told Wesley about UF, but had he found out somehow?

"Why would I be stressed?"

"Just because they haven't offered you a scholarship yet doesn't mean that they won't. It's still early."

I was finally able to exhale. He was still thinking about the scholarship. "Well, I don't just want to sit around hoping it comes through. Mr. King did that with the musical, and look what that got us." And just like that, an idea popped into my brain, and I slammed my hands down on the table. "That's it."

"What?"

"The project. Let's save the musical."

"As our project? Are you insane?"

"Why is that insane? Two birds with one stone."

"Jorie, we can't just 'save the musical.' Did you not hear me when I mentioned thousands?"

"Exactly. It's not going to be easy, but that's what will help us win. If we find a unique way to raise the money, we'll save the musical and impress the judges for the contest. It's win-win."

He looked weary, but he shrugged. "I guess it's got potential if it works."

"If I can impress UF and save the musical, then I'll consider that a success."

"You don't need to impress UF. You already got in."

I bit my lip. I didn't like lying to Wesley. In fact, I couldn't remember a time I'd ever lied to Wesley other than stupid childhood lies you tell when you're eight. I'd always been honest with Wesley, sometimes brutally so. When he had a big crush on Kim Selley, I crushed him by telling him that she thought he was dweeby. I probably could've lied then and saved his feelings, but what was the point? He had to know.

But now here I was lying to him about something I never thought I'd have to lie about. It felt wrong to lie to Wesley because I felt like I was breaking some kind of best friend code, but I just couldn't bear facing him. I'd bragged so much about UF. It seemed like a given. I just couldn't deal with however Wesley would react: pity, anger, gloating? It was hard to picture Wesley gloating, but regardless of his reaction, I didn't want to see it. I wouldn't be able to take the disappointment or pity on his face.

Luckily, his parents had convinced him to wait until he heard back on his other applications before committing to UT or I would have had to admit that I couldn't commit to UF on the same day as we had planned. I didn't know how I would ever tell him, so I was hoping that with the help of this project, I wouldn't have to.

"Come on, Wesley. You know this is a good idea."

He sighed. "Fine. But what can we do that will make a big enough difference? Mr. King has already canceled rehearsals. The set is being torn down next week."

"I don't think we have to get all the money upfront. If we get enough to keep it going and prove to Mr. Quentin and Mr. King that it's possible, I think they would let us move forward."

"And how are two high school seniors supposed to raise thousands of dollars in a couple of months?"

The bell rang, so we started packing up our bags to head to class. "I don't know, but I'm going to figure it out."

6

After I finished my homework, I spent the entire night researching fundraising methods. I looked into grants, I tried to find arts centers who donate, I even searched Pinterest for popular fundraising events. Everything was either completely unrealistic or not good enough. I hadn't hit that sweet spot yet of something that would be sufficient to produce the musical and impressive enough to wow UF without being completely unreasonable for Wesley and I to complete in a matter of weeks. The more research I did, the more I felt the possibility of pulling this off drifting away, and with it, any chance I had of getting into UF.

Maybe I just had to give up on the musical. Maybe trying to base our entire project around it was a waste of time and energy, and if we failed to save the musical, then there was no way it would be enough to win the competition, let alone impress UF. Plus, as sad as it would be, if the musical didn't happen, I'd have a lot more time to work on the government project, study for AP exams, pick up a few extra shifts, and actually enjoy senior year. But wasn't part of enjoying senior year doing the musical?

I clicked over to the tab that had my email to UF Admissions open. I wasn't sure what I thought would happen when I sent that email. I had sent it almost in a fit, a blur, and I didn't think about it. I was banking on this project getting me into UF, but what if it was meaningless? Maybe this wasn't what they wanted or wasn't enough, and I was doing it for nothing.

Not that the musical was nothing.

But I wasn't overly excited about doing all of this work if it didn't work. I had sent the email days ago, and still no one had responded. I had hoped they would reply. Even a form letter saying, "Thanks for the email, we'll take this new information into account, blah blah blah" would have alleviated some of the ever-rising anxiety I now had. Logically, I knew that UF Admissions must get millions of emails and so response times are slow, but I couldn't stop the intrusive side of my brain from convincing me that it meant that I wasn't doing enough, that *I* wasn't enough.

I shoved my laptop across the bed in frustration and pulled Taylor's paper on *Othello* from my backpack and started reading it. If I didn't finish reading this paper by tomorrow, she'd have my head. I had already put it off a day, but she had let it slide because of the musical fiasco. She wouldn't let it slide again.

Halfway through a paragraph about Iago being a sociopath, my dad knocked on my door a few times before opening.

"Busy?"

I shook my head. "Just reading Taylor's essay. What's up?"

He sat on the edge of my bed, but thinking better of it, stood and leaned against the door frame. Dad was always a little awkward all around when it came to having deep conversations with his teenage daughters, but it had been more than a little awkward for the past few days since the USF blowup. My parents and I hadn't spoken much beyond "Please set the table for dinner," and "Don't forget to buy the milk that Savannah likes."

"I just got an email from the school. The musical got shut down?" he asked, and I nodded. "What happened?"

"We lost our biggest sponsor, and without that money, the school can't afford to produce the musical."

"That's a real shame," he said. "I always enjoy seeing you perform. It's too bad that you'll miss out on your senior year musical."

"I'm not so ready to give up on it. I was trying to find a way to save it, but I don't know what to do."

"Oh honey, there might not be anything you can do."

"There has to be something. Besides, Wesley and I are working on this project for government class, and we need an idea, so I thought maybe this could be it. But Wesley isn't super invested in it, and I don't know how to save the musical, and if I can't, then I'll never—"

"Never what?"

I hadn't told my parents about UF, and I didn't think Savannah had either. They wouldn't understand. I'm not sure they would even care. They were all gung-ho for USF, so my not getting into UF would just be ammunition for their USF argument. I didn't want to hear the I-told-you-sos.

Finally, I said, "Nothing. Wesley and I just really want to win."

He moved his hand like he was about to say something, but he let it drop back down to his knee. He seemed to know that there was more to it that what I was telling him, but he chose not to call me on it. "So a fundraiser won't cut it?"

I shook my head. "We're going to need thousands. The usual fundraisers just won't bring in enough. I've been trying to come up with some kind of event we could host, like maybe the cast could do a few mini performances to raise interest, or we could host a fundraiser through Moe's or something, but I don't have the resources to organize that. Plus it would have to be an official organization to accept donations, especially if we want to win the competition."

"Why don't you start an organization then? You could start a non-profit."

I shook my head again. "I looked into that. We could start it, and I could cover the application costs with my savings, but we'd never get it officially approved by the IRS in time to save the musical."

This time, he did sit on the bed. "You don't need the approval to start collecting money. It's just a formality. As long as you do everything you're supposed to do, they'll approve it. I've helped start many nonprofits."

"Really? It's that easy?"

"Sure. You would just need a board, an application, and a name. I could help you with the application. Mom and I would even help cover the start-up costs."

"Thanks for the help with the application, but I'll cover the costs. I want to do this on my own. Well, with Wesley, of course."

Dad smiled. "That's our go-getter."

"And Dad?"

"Hmm?"

"I didn't mean to snap at you and Mom the other day."

"I know."

"I'll do the USF tour if she really wants me to."

He nodded. "I think it would mean a lot to her. It really is a good school. At least consider it before you make any final decisions."

I nodded, and Dad walked out, likely to go tell Mom that I had agreed to the tour, and I was left alone with my research. I still didn't want to go on that tour, but I decided it couldn't hurt anything. We'd go, we'd look at the school, and we'd leave. That's all it would be. At best, maybe Savannah would get something out of it since I knew she was interested. It didn't change anything. Walking the USF campus wouldn't change my mind. I was going to go to UF no matter what.

***

I spent the entire night researching nonprofits. It was a crazy idea—maybe even a little too crazy—but it was doable. It was a fairly simple application, and with my dad's help, I was confident I could complete it that weekend. There were some start-up costs: the application alone cost a few hundred and incorporating would be an additional cost, but I had been saving up my money from Moe's, and I could cover it. My dad had said that Wesley and I would need a board, but we didn't need a big one. I was pretty sure we could put that together quickly. It was possible.

But would it work? Mr. King had already tried to contact other potential donors and had come up empty. Other parents weren't willing to chip in. But maybe if they knew that the musical had been canceled? Maybe if a student asked them? Maybe if people knew how important the musical was to so many people, they would be more generous. I had to try. I wanted to save the musical for my friends, but if I was going to impress UF, then there was no question: I absolutely had to save it.

The next morning, I was waiting in the parking lot for Wesley to pull up. I wasn't sure how he was going to react to the idea—it would be a lot more work than I think he wanted out of this project—but I couldn't do this alone. I needed his help to pull it off. Really, I needed as much help as I could get. In an attempt at bribery, I had stopped at the Donutisserie to get him a large coffee and his favorite blueberry lemon donut. I could never understand why he liked that thing: I always thought it tasted sour.

While waiting for Wesley, Savannah said, "Do you really think Wesley is going to do whatever it is you want him to do just because you bought him coffee?"

"And the donut," I said. "Don't forget about the donut."

She rolled her eyes. "Because people can just be bought with pastries."

"You don't know Wesley like I do. Trust me, this will work."

"Ever thought about just asking him?"

"Shush," I said. "And go to class."

"Fine. Enjoy corrupting your friends."

"Will do," I called out as she walked away.

Wesley pulled into the spot next to me, and when he saw me holding the cup of coffee and the Donutisserie bag, he started laughing.

"Okay, what do you want?" He hopped out of his car and slung his backpack over his shoulder.

"I can't bring my best friend breakfast from his favorite donut shop without wanting something?" In response, he raised an eyebrow, so I handed him the objects of bribery. "Fine. I have an idea for the project."

"That's great," he said. "We need an idea. Why does that entail donuts?"

"I want to start a nonprofit organization to raise the money to save the musical."

Wesley choked a little on his coffee. "You want to *what*? Jorie, we're not on *Shark Tank*. We can't just start a business out of thin air."

I took his coffee and handed him a stack of papers with all the research I had done. I had made spreadsheets for timelines and costs, I had projections for goals we had to meet along the way, and I even had name suggestions. Wesley flipped through the pages, and I tried not to cringe visibly as he smeared lemon custard on some of them. He didn't speak the entire time he read, though he did give me a few side-eye glances. Finally, after a while, he traded me the papers for the coffee again.

"So?" I asked.

Wesley twisted his mouth. "I suppose it's possible. But Jorie, this is crazy. This will take so much time. And if we do succeed in saving the musical—"

"*When* we succeed."

"*If* we succeed, we'll be busy with rehearsals. I have a lead role. You're in the play and working backstage. Not to mention all of our normal classes, AP exam prep, prom committee, work, and everything else the two of us have going on combined. How on earth would we get this done?"

"I don't know, but we'll figure it out."

"I don't know. I was kind of just hoping for the extra credit from Ms. Corwin. I wasn't really trying to win."

"But think how good it'll look to UT if you do. And you still want the prize money, don't you?"

"I guess."

"And you want to be Gaston? Don't you want our senior musical to happen?"

"You know I do, but this is going to be a ton of work."

I shook my head. "It'll be manageable. We'll split the workload. We can even split it 60-40 or 70-30 if you want. I don't mind doing extra."

"Well, you already did all this research."

"Exactly."

Wesley sighed, and I knew I had talked him into it. "Okay. I'm willing to give it a try. But Jorie, if it doesn't work, we have to drop it. We can't sacrifice all this time and energy for nothing."

I stuck out my hand. "Deal." I would just have to make sure that it did work out. I would guarantee that the show would go on.

Wesley and I walked into the school past the elementary building as a shortcut. We weren't technically supposed to be walking on the elementary side of campus, but a lot of people did it as a shortcut. It was just faster to get to the science building that way. As long as you didn't get caught by the elementary principal, it was all good.

"Did you finish the lab report for chem?" I asked.

Wesley shook his head. "I'll finish during math class."

"Then when are you going to do your calculus homework?"

"During French."

"This is a slippery slope."

"I'm fine."

"I bet Ann does her homework on time," I said. "That's probably why she's beating you out for salutatorian."

Wesley smirked. "Shut up."

"This is why you think we don't have time to do the project: poor time management."

"You sound like my mom."

"Focus. Why couldn't we just come up with a name right now, while we walk?"

"Just pick one of the ones you already came up with. They're all good."

I scrunched my nose. "They're not good enough. They all sound either dumb or not important enough. We need something good."

"It's just a name. It's not that crucial."

"It's very crucial."

As we turned the corner, we heard a bit of a commotion. A bunch of little kids were squealing with excitement. As a K-12 school, we had all ages on the campus, and oddly enough, the kindergarten playground was in the center of campus. The little kids were always pretty hyper in the morning, but they seemed to be excited about something specific today. It took a minute to realize that they were crowded around Rachel. She must have been on her way to class when they spotted her. Rachel was smiling and trying her best to answer all of the questions that were being fired at her.

"Do you like singing?" one little girl with an oversized pink bow in her hair asked.

"I do."

"Do you sing all the time?"

Rachel shook her head with a smile. "Only sometimes."

A boy with white-blonde hair pulled gently on her arm. "You're my favoritest."

"Mine, too," several others chimed in.

"Aww, that's so sweet," Rachel said.

"Do you love the beast?" pink-bow girl asked.

Rachel turned the slightest bit pink. "He's definitely special. What do you think?"

Wesley leaned over and lowered his voice. "Do you think they know that she's not really Belle?"

I couldn't help but laugh. "Don't think so."

Another little girl with missing teeth beamed at Rachel. "I want to be just like you when I grow up."

"That's really nice of you to say," Rachel said, "but you should be just like you."

"But you're my hero," she said.

I grabbed Wesley's arm, and he jumped a little.

"What?" he asked.

"That's it."

"What's it?"

I pointed at the crowd around Rachel. "Look at that. Those kids look up to her just because she's the star of the musical. They don't even know Rachel, but they already look up to her. That little girl called Rachel her hero. That's our name."

"What, Rachel is a Hero dot com?"

I rolled my eyes. "No. Stage Heroes. Spotlight Heroes?"

Wesley snapped his fingers. "That one. Spotlight Heroes. I like it."

I wrote it down on my hand so that we wouldn't forget it. Spotlight Heroes. It was perfect. It showed that the musical was important to more than just the cast. The entire school was looking forward to the musical. The musical wasn't just for the Siennas of the world. It really was for all of us, and that was something people would be able to get behind.

7

—·—

Newly excited about our plan and our name, we headed to see Mr. King. We wouldn't be able to do this without his endorsement, and we had to convince him not to shut everything down completely yet. We still had a few minutes before first period, so we headed to his office.

"Mr. King," I said when I opened the door, "could Wesley and I talk to you for a minute?"

"The theater always has time for bright stars such as you."

"We have an idea that we'd like to run by you."

"What would that be?"

"We want to save the musical."

Mr. King smiled, but in that way adults always smile when they think that young people are incredibly naive. "Miss Haywood, Mr. Dixon, I, too, would love to save the musical. Unfortunately, the stars have not aligned."

Wesley said, "We understand, but we think we have an idea that will work. Will you hear us out?"

Mr. King hesitated, but motioned for us to continue. He was going to take more convincing than I originally thought.

We explained the project Ms. Corwin had offered and the stakes of winning the competition. We explained our nonprofit idea and detailed exactly how we would structure it. We showed him the projections I had created for hitting certain fundraising goals every two weeks. If we could meet those goals along the way, we would be able to cover costs as they came up. We could also hang on to our current sponsors by proving that the rest of the funds would come through. We needed sets before we needed costumes, which came before hiring the sound and lighting workers to manage the student volunteers, which we needed before playbills, and so on. We had a few ideas for fundraisers—bake sales, car washes, spirit nights at restaurants—and we promised more ideas when he looked skeptical. He hadn't shut us down yet, but he didn't look any more enthusiastic than he had when we first walked in, which wasn't much, if any at all.

"So?" Wesley asked. "What do you think?"

Mr. King studied the papers for a while before saying anything. After a few minutes, he set the papers down, closed his eyes, and held his hands in a prayer position against his mouth. He always did this when choreographing our musicals. Wesley once asked him what he was doing, and he said something about a muse. No one ever asked again.

"Perhaps my biggest concern is the cost. Your projections are too low."

"They are?" I asked. "I did some research, and this seemed normal."

He nodded. "For certain plays, it is, especially plays. But the rights to a musical are more expensive, and the scale is so much grander in order to do it well. You both have known me long enough to know that I have high expectations for our productions."

We did know. Mr. King didn't do anything halfway. We could probably produce a perfectly good musical for less than Mr. King wanted, but he would never go for it. He had extremely high standards, and no one could doubt that he offered results, but I started to worry about the cost. I had crunched the numbers, and I thought I had allotted enough allowance for Mr. King's expectations, but he was already doubting. Maybe I was getting myself in over my head.

"So how much do we need to raise total?"

Mr. King hesitated only briefly. "At least $5,000." That was nearly double what I had projected. "It isn't as bad as it sounds. I already paid for the rights, which was more than a grand. I had some more money pledged from our usual sponsors, but most of them dropped out the moment that Bill Bunton dropped out. I'm not sure if they'll come through without him."

"But what if they see that we are raising the money? If there's even a chance that the rest of the funding could come through, wouldn't they still commit?"

He shrugged. "Maybe. I certainly hope so."

"And couldn't we get parent donors?"

"The parents will only donate if the musical is a guarantee. In past years, they were more willing, but I don't have to tell you how the economy is not what it was."

Times were tough, and small towns were struggling more than most. What if we couldn't convince parents to donate when times were tough? The economy wasn't our fault, of course, but we couldn't pretend that it wasn't a factor.

Wesley shifted forward on his chair. "Mr. King, when Jorie sets her mind to something, it's pretty much a guarantee."

I couldn't help but smile. It was nice to know that Wesley always believed in me no matter what. I wondered if he would still feel that way if he knew about UF. I had set my mind to that, and it had completely fallen apart.

Mr. King smiled also. "Jorie is certainly a powerful wave, but you're talking about tackling a monster greater than Goliath."

"Can't we at least try?" I asked. "We've got nothing to lose. If it doesn't work, then nothing's changed. But if we can hit those first few goals, we would have a real shot."

"I'm willing to let you run with it, but if I assume that you will succeed, then I have to resume rehearsals. If I get everyone on board again, it will be more devastating if I have to cancel a second time. It won't look good for me or for you."

He was right, of course, but I had to try. I had to take that risk if I had any hope of saving the musical or, more importantly, saving my chances at UF. I might have been committing social suicide by risking getting everyone's hopes up just to dash them, but would that be worse than everyone finding out I didn't get into UF?

Wesley looked to me for an answer, so I tried to smile with confidence. "I'll take that chance if you will."

Mr. King covered his mouth, but I swore that I saw him smile. "Mr. Quentin will take some convincing. You'll have to hit that first fundraising goal if I have any chance of convincing him to let this move forward."

"So, is that a yes?"

"That is an emphatic and resounding yes."

"Thank you, Mr. King," Wesley said, shaking his hand. "We'll keep you up to date as we go."

"Please do."

We left his office and high-fived in the hallway. We were on our way to pulling this off. Maybe, just maybe, we could actually save the musical, win the competition, and then UF would see that they had made a mistake. Maybe no one, including Wesley, would ever have to know that I got waitlisted. This could actually work.

The only thing stopping us was the number. Ten grand was higher than either of us had thought, but since Mr. King had greenlit the idea, we had to pull it off. Ms. Corwin would likely help, but I wanted Wesley and I to have more to go on before we asked for her help. I wanted to impress her.

"I can't believe he actually went for it," Wesley said as we walked down the hallway.

"Of course he did. It's a fantastic idea."

"You were fantastic," he said, cheeks flushed, then abruptly turned his face away from me.

What was that?

"So," he continued after he cleared his throat, "we need to plan our first fundraiser, right?"

"Right," I said, though the air in the hall felt different suddenly. What had just shifted?

***

I headed to see Ms. Corwin after our meeting with Mr. King. I didn't want to ask for her help, but Wesley and I still hadn't officially informed her that we were entering, though I thought she knew somehow. Wesley had offered to come with me, but I kind of wanted to tell her on my own. She'd always been so supportive of me, and I wanted to uphold that.

Lunch was about to start, so I had a window to catch her before she had another class. I found her in her classroom, and when she saw me, she waved at me to enter.

"Good afternoon, Miss Haywood. What can I do for you?"

I held out the typed proposal I'd put together the night before. I wasn't sure if a proposal was necessary, but I decided it couldn't hurt. "Wesley and I would like to enter the competition."

She smiled. "Crossroads of Education and Government? That's wonderful. I'm so glad you reconsidered. What changed your mind?"

A complete and utter rejection that was so upsetting that I became desperate. "It just made sense, I guess. I was worried about the workload at first, but Wesley—Wesley and I decided it would be beneficial for both of us."

"I think it will be. A formal proposal, very impressive."

I pointed at a few of the pages where I had made revisions in pen. "Unfortunately, it isn't perfect. I met with Mr. King this morning, and I had to change some of the numbers I had typed up last night."

"That's all right. I'll submit the application for you both right away." She skimmed the pages, nodding the entire time. "This is an exciting idea. We were all very sad to hear that the musical wouldn't happen. I'm so glad to see some of my most diligent students taking matters into their own hands."

"Well, it's more complicated than we initially thought."

"How so?"

"Money." I shrugged my shoulders lazily.

"Ah, yes. The plight of many. Any ideas?"

"We've got a few."

"If I can help in any way, please let me know. Obviously I can't help you with the project itself because that wouldn't be fair, but if you need teacher authorization for anything or contact information for anyone, I'm happy to help."

"Thank you," I said, glancing down.

"Jorie, are you all right? You seem a little down."

My eyes darted to meet hers, which were filled with concern. "I'm fine. It's just early."

She stared. "You're sure?"

"I'm sure."

"Well, I hear from murmurs that you got into UF. That's wonderful news. I'm very happy for you."

My hands fidgeted behind my back. "Thank you."

She held up the proposal. "Do you mind if I hold onto this for a day or so so I can look it over?"

"Not at all. Go ahead. I'll see you later," I said, turned right around, and walked out before she could stop me.

I had lied to Wesley, to Sienna, to Taylor, and now to Ms. Corwin. Countless people at this school thought I had gotten into UF, and I was letting them think that. Heck, I was *encouraging* them to think that. Everything was snowballing. Was I just digging a deeper hole? How deep did the hole have to get before I wouldn't be able to find a way out of it, and had I already passed that point?

***

During study hall, Wesley and I tried to hammer out the details. We had picked a name already—or rather, I had picked a name since I had been the one to come up with Spotlight Heroes and Wesley had just agreed to it—but we had to figure out exactly what we would do to raise the money. Mr. King's number was high, and my projected biweekly goals had jumped quite a bit, so the usual bake sales were not going to cut it: we needed something big. Maybe a few big somethings. We had a few ideas, but I wasn't sure that any of them were good enough. Plus, we still hadn't been able to organize a board. My parents had offered, but I wanted something more official than just our parents. And less lame.

Wesley tapped his pencil on the table for so long that I had the indescribable urge to rip it out of his hand and throw it across the room. Why do people enjoy tapping pencils? It's so annoying.

"Maybe if we go door to door?" he said.

"What, like girl scouts? We'll never make any money that way."

"If we go around the rich neighborhoods, maybe."

"They won't even answer the door for us."

"Isn't that the point of the nonprofit? Isn't that supposed to bring in extra money?"

I laughed. "It doesn't just do that magically. You have to plan events or other fundraisers."

"Then why do we need Spotlight Heroes?"

"Because it makes everything official. This way we're not just some random high school kids collecting money. This makes us legit. Besides, it will look cooler to the judges that we didn't just fundraise, which anyone could do, but we actually created our own business."

He shrugged. "I guess so."

"You don't agree?"

"No, I do, but the more we can't come up with ideas, the more worried I get about the work involved in this."

"Stop stressing about it. It'll be fine."

I started googling fundraising ideas, but they were all the same. Maybe Wesley was right. Maybe this would never work. We needed to raise enough to convince Mr. Quentin not to shut this down, and we would definitely need more ideas if we were going to put a board together that would be willing to support us. I might have bitten off more than either of us could chew, but could I really give up now? I had to get into UF before anyone found out what had really happened.

As if on cue, Sienna sauntered over to our table and smiled. "Hey, you two," she said. "What are you working on?"

"Nothing," I said.

Wesley chimed in, "The government project. The one Ms. Corwin offered."

"The AutoMall one?" she said with more than a hint of disdain. "You guys are actually entering that?"

"Yeah," Wesley said despite my kick to his leg under the table. Why do guys never recognize when girls are being mean? "Extra credit, you know?"

Sienna laughed. "You two hardly need extra credit."

"It's not that we need it," I said. "We're trying to do something good."

"Well, I want the extra credit," Wesley said.

Sienna flipped her hair, causing her bangles to tinkle. "Fair enough. Oh Jorie, I keep forgetting to ask you. I pestered my dad a little to see if he could get my name listed for early registration at UF. As a major donor, he can do things like that." Another hair flip. *Ugh.* "He thought I was being selfish, so I offered to get you on the list too, but he couldn't find your name."

My skin suddenly turned to ice, and yet, I was aware that I was sweating. I cleared my throat in an attempt to sound casual, but it sounded anything but. "That's weird."

Sienna nodded. "Yeah it was. I thought maybe he was spelling your name wrong. You know, maybe he wasn't putting in 'Marjorie' or something, but it still didn't come up. Why don't you give me your ID number? I can still get you on the list."

"That's okay, you really don't have to do that." I wanted to run away, but of course, that wasn't an option.

"Really, I insist."

"Sienna, it's fine, really. Besides, I don't know my ID number off the top of my head."

"Really? Ever since my acceptance, I've had to put it in a million times to fill everything out." A devious smile crossed her lips, and I knew that I was through. "Wait, did you not get in?"

"Of course she did," Wesley said in an attempt to be helpful, but of course he only made it worse. When I didn't say anything, Wesley gave me a weird look. "Jorie?"

"Oh my goodness," Sienna said. "You actually didn't get in, did you? You mean I got into UF, and you didn't? You know, I thought your reaction in class the day the letters came out was a little weird. I can't believe you didn't get in. Wow, no wonder my dad couldn't find your name. That's crazy. So what are you going to do now? Did you apply anywhere else? I thought you only applied to UF. Oh no, what if you didn't get in anywhere else? That would be awful. Why did you say you got in? Had you not heard yet?"

Wesley interrupted Sienna's tirade. "Jorie?"

I slammed my palms on the table and stood up. "Of course I got in. I'm just not doing early registration. Not all of our parents can just pay money to a school to get special privileges."

"Jorie," Wesley said with a warning tone.

But it was like I couldn't stop myself. It was like the words were just exploding out of my mouth before I could even think about what a horrendously bad idea they were. And with every word that flooded out in a nearly hysterical rage, I felt the knot in my stomach growing bigger and tighter.

"Besides, Wesley and I are kind of busy trying to save the musical that you claim to care about. So when we do save it and you get your moment on stage as a senior, you can thank us. Even though I know you won't because you never think about anyone but yourself."

"Jorie," Wesley practically snapped though his voice was quiet. Sienna let her mouth hang open, and like a scene from a bad teen drama, she spun on her heels and stomped off in a huff. Once she was gone, Wesley put his hand on my arm. "What was that?"

"It's fine," I said. "I've got to go talk to Ms. Corwin about our project. I'll see you later, Wesley."

And with that, I left the library as quickly as I possibly could. I didn't want to talk to anyone right now. I knew Wesley would follow me eventually, so I ducked into the restroom and sat on the bench in the corner.

I tried to stop it, but I felt the tears run down the side of my face in a complete and utter betrayal of my own will. Wesley was already texting me "Where are you?" but I just turned off the ringer and shoved my phone in my bag. He was probably just worried about me, wondering why I blew up like that, but I couldn't tell him. I couldn't let him or Sienna or anyone know. He would be so mad that I didn't tell him. Or worse, he would pity me.

I felt a little like throwing up. If I had eaten anything that morning, I might have.

8

You know you're really upset when neither *Friends* nor *Gilmore Girls* can cheer you up. I'd watched at least five episodes of each since last night, and I didn't feel any better. In an effort to drown out my own thoughts, I'd cranked up the volume so loudly that I didn't even hear Savannah knocking over the booming of the *Friends* theme song until she banged on the door so violently I thought she might break the doorknob from trying to force my door open—again.

"Hey Grandma," Savannah said as she threw the door open, "could you dial down your cheesy sitcoms in here? Some of us are trying to study."

"They're not cheesy, and you're not studying."

"Well, it's still annoying."

"I don't care. Now go away."

"Why?"

"Because I never actually told you that you could come in."

Savannah wrinkled her nose. "Anyway, Wesley is here."

I bolted upright. "What? Why didn't you say something sooner?"

"I tried, but your TV was blasting."

"How long has he been here?"

"Couple minutes."

"Why?"

"Because that's how long ago he got here."

I glared at her. "Why is he here?"

"Oh-em-gee, I'm not your messenger. Why don't you find out yourself?"

"You're grouchy today."

"Right back atcha." Savannah shut my door, and I heard her say something to Wesley.

I rushed over to my mirror, rubbed the smudged mascara off my face, brushed my hair, and changed out of my disreputable donut pajama pants and into slightly less disreputable yoga pants. I wasn't totally sure that I wanted to see Wesley, but since he was in my house, I didn't really have a choice.

I froze for a second. Why did I care how I looked in front of Wesley in my own house? He'd been over a million times before, and I had never worried about it. I forced myself to relax a little. It was just Wesley, after all.

I peeked around the corner from my bedroom and saw Wesley sitting at our breakfast bar, eating one of the muffins my mom made last night.

"Already made your way into the Haywood family muffin stash, I see."

Wesley practically jumped three feet in the air, and muffin crumbs went flying. He furiously chomped on his mouthful of muffin and swallowed hard.

"You know I can't ignore your mom's orange zest muffins."

"What are you doing here?"

"I wanted to make sure you were okay. You seemed upset the other day, and I was worried about you."

I tried to shrug casually. "Just Sienna getting under my skin, that's all."

"You don't usually let Sienna get to you like that. Is something wrong?"

Savannah cleared her throat behind Wesley, but thankfully, he didn't notice. I knew I should tell him, but I just couldn't. I had already lied to him twice, and I just couldn't face his reaction, whatever it would be. If this project worked out, maybe I never would have to tell him.

I forced a smile. "I'm fine. It was just a stressful day, and Sienna was the last thing I needed. I just really want this project to work."

Wesley sat up a little straighter. "About that. I've made an executive decision."

"What's that?"

"I've decided that if we're going to be successful, then we can't stress ourselves out too much. We need to relax. And I know just what to do."

I folded my arms, but I couldn't stop the smirk that jumped onto my face. "Oh do you?"

Wesley nodded his head. "I'm just too good of a friend to let you work yourself to death on this thing, and we both know that you will if I let you. So we're going out."

"Out where?"

Wesley pulled out a red plastic tiara that was covered in glitter and shaped by the images of strawberries. "Two words: Strawberry Festival."

The Strawberry Festival was the most absurd thing you could possibly imagine. Central Florida was known for its strawberry harvest, and we actually had an entire festival devoted to strawberries. That was the kind of thing small towns did for entertainment. It was exactly how it sounded, too. Almost all of the food had strawberries, the rides were strawberry-themed, and there was even a strawberry mascot that walked around the festival. It was the most ridiculous thing you could possibly imagine—and yet, it was one of my favorite things to do all year.

I pointed at the crown. "You can't possibly expect me to wear that out in public."

"Well you better, because I've got a matching strawberry king crown, and I'll look stupid wearing that by myself."

"Oh, because it won't look stupid together?"

"Of course it will, but that's the fun part."

I squinted. "There's not even a strawberry king."

"Until now."

***

Wesley drove us to the festival, and it was slightly awkward at first. It was like we could both sense the tension between us, but neither of us was willing to acknowledge that it existed. Instead, after a prolonged period of awkward silence filled only by periodic casual conversation, he plugged in his phone and cranked his country music playlist. We had always disagreed over what actually qualified as country—I was more welcoming of the current pop-infused country, but he was a George Strait purist—but he had slipped some Luke Bryan and Kelsea Ballerini into the list, likely for me. We rolled down the windows and screamed the lyrics as loudly as we could, and it felt so good, like the synchronicity of belting lines about driving backroads while actually driving down slightly sketchy backroads was healing to the soul.

This was why Wesley and I were friends. We understood each other in a way that no one else did. That time that Kim had totally rejected him, I called him and demanded that he pick me up from work. It was before I bought my truck, and my mom had dropped me off at work. He hadn't wanted to come, but I guilt tripped him that he didn't care about my safety, so finally he came. I made him stop at McDonald s, claiming that I was hungry, and ordered a large M&M McFlurry for him. The second I ordered it, he had cracked a tiny smile, and I had officially broken through his slump. For Wesley, there was nothing an M&M McFlurry couldn't fix. We almost never actually talked about whatever was upsetting one or both of us. We just fixed it with the silliest things: with cheap milkshakes, drives down backroads, country music, late night waffles, or Disney movie nights. It always worked.

I looked over at Wesley, who was unaware of my staring because he was belting out some Carrie Underwood like a champ, and thought about how silly I was being. Why couldn't I tell him about UF? When had I ever not told him absolutely everything that was on my mind? When had I ever not been honest with him? It was absurd. Wesley would understand. *Of course* Wesley would understand. And right now, I needed someone to understand. I needed someone in my corner, and Wesley had never been anywhere else. But not here. I wasn't about to drop that bomb while we were driving down a dirt road. Later.

We paid an exorbitant amount of money to park in one of the closer lots and made a beeline for the best strawberry shortcake stand at the entire festival. As per usual, Wesley mocked me for putting an excessive amount of whipped cream on mine, and I mocked him for getting a biscuit instead of the pound cake, and we ate shortcake until our stomachs hurt.

While waiting for our stomachs to settle, we flopped onto a bench in the shade. Wesley pulled the crowns out of the backpack he always brought to the festival to sneak in contraband water bottles to avoid paying and handed me the red tiara.

"The time has come," he said.

"I thought you were kidding."

Wesley mocked insult. "I *never* kid about strawberry crowns. Come on, Haywood, embrace the crown."

He tucked the clips of the tiara behind my ears, and even though he'd probably touched my hair a million times before to pick something out of it or brush it out of his face for pictures, it felt weirdly different this time. I wasn't exactly sure what I felt, but seeing his face so close to mine while he fidgeted with my hair to get the tiara just right made my lungs feel a little heavy.

"Perfect," he said, and held up his phone camera as a mirror for me.

I laughed when I saw myself. "Okay, it's official: redheads should definitely not wear red strawberry crowns."

"Oh, I don't know. I think we might be on to something. You're rocking that harder than the strawberry queen."

"Yeah, right. Have you seen the strawberry queen walking around? She's gorgeous."

"I stand by my earlier statement." And again, there was that heaviness in my chest.

An elderly couple walked over to us as we were taking a selfie and smiled wide. They were that kind of elderly couple that you dream about being someday because they were just so cute. They were wearing matching strawberry T-shirts, and they held hands and smiled at each other like it was the first time they had ever seen each other.

The woman said, "Oh, you two look so precious. Would you like us to take a picture for you?"

"Sure," Wesley said and jumped up as I handed my phone to her.

We struck a silly pose, and the woman's husband photobombed us, which only made us laugh harder. She kept snapping pictures the entire time that we laughed, he photobombed, Wesley shouted "All hail the king and queen," and I felt tears streaming down my face from laughing. People walking by were definitely watching and laughing at us, but I almost didn't care. I knew that the four of us were definitely having the most fun out of anyone at the festival.

They introduced themselves as Barbara and Edward, and we bought the couple some donuts and soda as a thank-you for a good time, both of them accepting cheerfully.

"No, thank you," Barbara said. "This is the most fun we've had at the festival in years."

I smiled. "Us, too."

She took my arm and pulled me just out of earshot of her husband and Wesley, who were talking about whether or not the Tampa Bay Lightning would go all the way this year. "You know, you and your friend remind me of Edward and me when we were your age."

"What do you mean?"

"Oh we've been together since we were seventeen. Our families lived next door to each other growing up. We've been best friends for more than fifty years. That's the foundation of a good relationship, you know. After all this time, we still enjoy each other because we're best friends."

I turned a little red. "Oh, Wesley and I aren't together, ma'am. We're just really good friends. Have been since grade school."

She smiled. "That's just what Edward and I used to say."

Edward walked over. "Are you ready to get going, honey bunny?"

Wesley and I tried in vain to suppress our laughter at the pet name.

"Have a wonderful day, you two!" Barbara called out as they walked away.

Wesley put his hands on his lower back and chuckled. "Ready for more food?"

"Oh you bet."

We ate our weight in donuts, strawberries, turkey legs, funnel cake, a variety of deep fried desserts, and washed it all down with more lemonade and root beer than could possibly be healthy. We dared each other to eat deep fried pickles and competed to see who could down a glass of the nasty strawberry soda the fastest.

We watched the pig races and rode the tamer rides that wouldn't make us lose all the food we had eaten, and listened outside the gates of the concert as Scotty McCreery sang since we didn't want to pay for tickets. It was the perfect day.

We'd done this a million times before. Wesley and I had always had a lot of fun together. When we were kids, our parents used to joke that they couldn't keep us apart. We'd competed over gross novelty sodas, eaten too much sugar, stood outside concerts, and sweated in the Florida sun countless times before, but I couldn't help but think that it felt different this time. I caught myself watching his mouth when he laughed, staring at his arms when he threw softballs at milk bottles, feeling flushed when he laughed. I'd always known that Wesley was good-looking—heck, most of River Glen knew that—but I had never noticed like *this*. I had never felt anything deep down inside when noticing those things before.

I spent most of the day trying to convince myself that I shouldn't be thinking those things, that I shouldn't be *feeling* those things when looking at Wesley. We were best friends, after all. This was textbook: best friends should never date because the relationship and therefore the friendship ends. But it seemed that now that I had noticed the way my head felt fuzzy when I looked at him that I couldn't not notice it any longer. And so, no matter what crazy activity he suggested next, I always agreed, eager to see what would happen next.

I couldn't remember the last time I'd had this much fun. I'd been so stressed out for months over college applications and classwork and work that I had forgotten to enjoy senior year. Wesley and I hadn't hung out like this in weeks. I resolved that I would make an effort to have some fun for the rest of the year. Wesley, Taylor, and I would have to have friend nights more often. After all, we would be heading off to college soon. Taylor planned to go out of state, Wesley would be in Tampa, and I would be—

Where would I be?

I had managed to forget about everything for a while today because we were having so much fun. It was nice not thinking about it. I could feel the sadness and anxiety creeping back in, and I was determined not to let that happen at least until tomorrow. Tomorrow, I would tell him everything. I wouldn't ruin this perfect day.

We were kind of just wandering around, and I desperately needed a distraction from this self-inflicted guilt trip. When I spotted the Ferris wheel, I gripped Wesley's arm, and he jumped.

"Ah! What? Why are you permanently scarring my arm?"

"Let's go on the Ferris wheel," I said.

His eyes got huge. "Not on your life, Haywood."

"Oh come on, Dixon, don't be such a wimp."

"Not wanting to ride a rickety festival ride is not being a wimp."

"Okay, fair enough. But come on. It'll be fine." Wesley looked unconvinced. "For me?"

He sighed heavily. "Fine."

The sun was starting to set, and since a majority of the people were starting to leave at that point, the line for the Ferris wheel wasn't very long. We got on the first round, and Wesley's knuckles were already turning white from gripping the lap bar.

"Dude, we're not even more than a few feet off the ground yet," I said. "You've got to relax."

He laughed nervously. "I'll relax when we're back on the ground."

We started to go higher, and when we were about halfway, we both realized simultaneously that sunset is the absolute worst time to ride a Ferris wheel. The sun pierced into our eyes, and we both shot our arms up to shield our faces.

"Great idea, Jorie," Wesley said. "Riding a Ferris wheel at sunset. Brilliant."

"Hey, you could have said something too, you know."

"I did! I'm not the one that wanted to be on this death-trap."

"You didn't say anything about the sun."

Now we can experience retina damage before we plunge to our deaths. How festive."

"Don't be so dramatic." I slumped down a little in a futile attempt to hide from the sun and felt the tiara bump against the railing. "Oh wow, I forgot I was wearing this."

"How could you forget that fine piece of headwear?"

"We should have gotten Barbara and Edward matching crowns. That really would have made our pictures."

Wesley laughed, naturally this time, for the first time since we'd gotten on the Ferris wheel. I felt the heaviness in my chest once more. "That would have been festive, for sure."

Barbara's words drifted into my ears again as clearly as if she had been speaking them at that moment: *That's just what Edward and I used to say.* Wesley hadn't heard her: he'd been talking to Edward at the time. Did I dare tell him? I couldn't help but wonder what he would think. I had a strange desire to see his reaction, and yet, I also didn't want to know his reaction. If he reacted favorably, what did that mean? And if he didn't react favorably, what did *that* mean? And what did I consider a favorable reaction?

I decided just to bite the bullet. "You know, she said the funniest thing to me right before they left."

"What's that?"

I fidgeted with the hem of my shirt. "She said we reminded her of her and Edward. When they were young, I mean."

Wesley looked puzzled. Was that a good or a bad reaction? "That's weird. Did she say why?"

"They grew up together, too. She said they actually lived next door to each other."

"Wouldn't that be convenient. I wouldn't have to drive across town to pick you up and force you to attend the Strawberry Festival."

I laughed, but I was determined now to get it all out. "She said that they didn't realize they liked each other until the end of high school. I think she thought you and I were together."

Did Wesley just blush? "Huh. That's interesting. What did you say?"

Suddenly I wasn't sure which one of us was waiting for a certain reaction from the other. "I said we weren't together, that we were just good friends. She said, 'That's what Edward and I used to say.'"

Wesley didn't laugh that time, and he didn't seem to be gripping the lap bar anymore. "And what did you say to that?"

"I didn't really say anything. You guys walked over. Isn't that weird of her to say though? Like just out of the blue?"

Wesley hesitated. "Is it?"

I dropped the hem of my shirt and forced myself not to break eye contact, and I couldn't help but notice that I really liked staring into his deep blue eyes. Was he saying what I thought he was saying? "What?"

Wesley shrugged ever so slightly. "Is it that weird? I mean, would it be weird?"

"I'm not sure." That, at least, was an honest answer.

The Ferris wheel jerked a little bit, and a moment of fear flashed across Wesley's eyes, but he chuckled and refocused quickly. He shifted a little closer to me since the jerk had bumped him over, reached his arm out across the seat behind me, and stared straight into my eyes. I wasn't totally sure what he was thinking, but strangely and unexpectedly, I found myself hoping for a very specific outcome. When his gaze dropped from my eyes to my lips, I felt my heart rate jump and felt pretty sure that I wasn't just sweating from the Florida heat anymore.

He lifted the hand that wasn't across the seat back to my chin, just letting his fingertips graze the back of my neck. Every touch of his hand felt like a spark. He seemed to watch the trail of his fingers along my neck. Finally, he leaned in and kissed me, not softly, not strongly, but just right. I could smell the remains of cologne he must have put on that morning and wondered how I hadn't noticed that before. Cologne at the Strawberry Festival? Had he planned for this to happen, *wanted* this to happen?

He shifted his hand, and chills ran down my arms. I didn't want it to end, but I didn't know how to keep it going, so I placed my hand on his wrist and hoped against hope it would always stay this way.

The seat jerked again, and Wesley pulled back, a little tense, and laughed again. His hand gripped the seat back, but he didn't move his left hand off of my chin, and I was grateful for that.

"I don't know why I'm trying to do this on a rickety Ferris wheel," he said with a chuckle. "Seems like a bad idea."

I shook my head. "It was perfect."

He smiled that handsome smile, that smile that would make just about anyone smile, and settled against the chair back again. He hadn't moved the arm resting behind me, so I settled in against his chest and, after a moment of hesitation, I let my head rest on his shoulder. He was warm, maybe a little overly warm from the sun beating down on us, but I didn't mind. I glanced down and noticed what looked like powdered sugar on the bottom of his shirt that must have landed there after his second funnel cake. It was such an inconsequential detail that noticing it gave me the inappropriate urge to laugh out loud, but I didn't. Instead, I smiled at the warmth I felt when Wesley shifted his arm down off the seat back to rest around my shoulder.

The chair jerked once again, but this time, he didn't flinch.

9

It had been two days since the Strawberry Festival.

Two days since I had spoken to Wesley.

Two days since I had *kissed* Wesley. Wesley. Wesley Dixon. My best friend since third grade. How on earth could I have kissed him?

Technically, he kissed me.

And more importantly, why hadn't we spoken since it happened? I mean, it's not like we text every single weekend, but I would have thought that after kissing and completely redefining our relationship and potentially jeopardizing our friendship that texting would be the absolute bare minimum of what we would do.

I couldn't help but wonder if he regretted it. We didn't talk a whole lot on the drive home from the festival. He made a few jokes, I laughed, he asked if I had a good time, I thanked him for getting me out of my head, and that was pretty much it. He certainly didn't kiss me when he dropped me off at home. Had I wanted him to kiss me goodnight? Of course I had. But did it mean anything that he hadn't done it?

I suppose I could have texted him, but I felt kind of weird about it, like he should be the one to initiate it since he's the one who had initiated the Ferris wheel make-out session. I must have typed a million drafts to Taylor to ask her for her opinion, but I hadn't been able to bring myself to send any of them. Taylor would freak if she knew.

Besides, what was I going to say to him? I still hadn't told him the truth. I'd been perfectly content with my decision to tell him everything the next day, but then he had to go and kiss me and ruin everything. Now it was going to be nearly impossible to tell him.

And that was the reason that I was at the school parking lot twenty minutes before I normally got there. I wanted to be there when Wesley arrived so that I could gauge his reaction when he saw me. Would he be happy, try to avoid me, the same as always? I had to know.

Savannah groaned in the front seat next to me. "Why are we here so Early."

"It's not that early. Don't be such a baby."

"There's literally no reason for us to be here this early."

"Would you chill?"

"Would you let me sleep in?"

"Too late now, so get over it."

Savannah didn't say anything for a few minutes, and I was grateful. I didn't want to hear her whining, and I definitely didn't want Wesley to arrive before I had carefully crafted what I would say to him when he showed up. I had to be prepared. Despite all of my inward panicking, I was determined to appear calm.

"So did you and Wesley have a fight or something?" Savannah asked.

"Nosey."

"Well you went to the festival with him on Saturday, and you've been weird ever since. I assume you had a fight."

"We didn't have a fight."

"Really? He wasn't even mad that you didn't tell him about UF?"

I whipped my head around. "No."

Savannah sat up. "You still haven't told him?"

"Go back to pouting about it being early."

"Jorie, you have to tell him."

"Just stay out of my business."

She was quiet for a moment, then said, "So you're just never going to tell him? You're going to lie to him forever? What are you going to do, move to Gainesville, buy a UF shirt, and live a lie?"

"Holy cow, stop with the questions."

Savannah pointed out the window. "Fine. I see Audrey pulling up. I'll leave you to your moodiness."

"Thank goodness."

Savannah left, and I was finally able to think more clearly. I would definitely say hi when he pulled up. Should I get out of my car and wait? No, that's weird. When he pulled up, I'd get out and say hi, just like I always did. Then I could see how he reacted.

But when would be the right moment to tell him? There probably wasn't one.

I knew what I wanted him to say. Or, at least I thought I did. I didn't want pity. *That* was for sure. I didn't want sympathetic statements about how "everything would turn out all right," and unfortunately, Wesley was just nice enough to offer such niceties.

I wanted some kind of understanding for the lie. We'd been friends a long time. It wasn't like this was the first time we'd ever lied to each other. Though I had to admit it hadn't really been since we were kids. Of all people, I hoped Wesley would understand that I had panicked, *why* I had panicked. He was usually pretty reasonable when it came to things like this. Maybe there would even be another kiss involved. Who knew? He would understand, right?

My phone buzzed, and I inexplicably hoped that it was Wesley even though I knew he was likely driving, but it was just Taylor asking how I was doing. We hadn't really talked at all over the weekend.

I still hadn't told Taylor either. Somehow, I thought she kind of knew. She was there when the decisions came out, and she'd seen me act kind of strangely. I felt like she was just waiting for me to admit it. Would she tell Wesley if I did? Would she tell him her suspicions anyway? Maybe she already had, and that was the real reason Wesley had taken me out—it had been nothing more than a distraction. That was a depressing thought.

I stared at my phone for a while trying to figure out what to say to Taylor. I could just ignore it and talk to her in person. But what if we couldn't get alone, away from eavesdroppers? But how could I possibly explain everything in just a few words? And how could I talk to her without talking about Wesley?

I was so engrossed in my text dilemma, that I completely missed Wesley pulling in. I made eye contact with him, and he was smiling, but the car was already in park. How long had he been there watching me stare at my phone? And when did he start smiling?

I got out of the car and smiled as nonchalantly as I could, but in reality, I wanted to scream just to fill the awkward void with something tangible and real, something beyond this guessing game of does he or doesn't he. He turned back for a second seeming like he forgot something in his car and grabbed two coffee cups from the Donutisserie and held one out to me.

I looked at it but didn't take it. "Are you trying to bribe me?" Good, yeah, that sounded natural.

"No. Why would you think that?"

"Because I brought you Donutisserie coffee to bribe you into the project."

"I thought you just understood my inherent need for coffee on a spiritual level."

I couldn't stop the smirk on my face. "Shut up."

He held out the cup closer to me. "So, are you going to take your weird chai drink?"

I took the drink and thanked him, but I couldn't help feeling like this was normal. This was how Wesley and I always acted. Shouldn't it be different? Shouldn't the immensity hanging over us have some kind of impact?

We had started walking toward the school, and if I was going to say anything, I had to do it now before we got inside the school, and I would no doubt run into Sienna who would corner us again. If I had any chance of clearing anything up, the time was now. It would have been awkward to have this conversation over text after all.

"So," Wesley said before I got the chance, "I've got a question for you."

"Ah, so this is bribe coffee."

He scrunched his face. "It's not even coffee, and it's not a bribe. It's a genuine question."

"Shoot."

"I wanted to ask you about the project."

Not what I was hoping for. "The project?"

He nodded. "I wasn't sure if you still wanted to do it."

Did he not want to do it? Did he not want to spend that much extended time together? "Why wouldn't I?"

"I don't know." He gave the shoulder not supporting his backpack a little shrug. "I wasn't sure. You seemed kind of off the other day, and I thought maybe you felt like it was too much pressure or something. It kind of seemed like you did it as a favor to me, but it's not that big of a deal if you want to drop it. I feel a little bit like I forced you into it."

I never told him I didn't get into UF. I never told him I wanted to do the government project to salvage my chances of getting off the waitlist. I should have told him why I wanted to do the project. He probably would've understood. He would probably still understand now.

But I said, "I want to save the musical," and it was at least true, even if it was leaving out the most important piece of information. But how could I tell him now that I wanted to do the project solely for myself, not because I wanted to help him out or do him some kind of favor? Everything felt different now. A few minutes on a Ferris wheel had completely changed everything.

"So you're still in?"

Without thinking, I stuck out my hand for a handshake. "Still in if you are."

He accepted the handshake, and we'd probably shaken hands a million times before, but this time, I felt that little spark I felt on Saturday when his fingers touched my chin. I wondered if he felt it, too. When it felt like he tugged on my arm a little bit, I was convinced that he did, convinced he was about to pull me in and kiss me, but as quickly as I thought it, he dropped my hand, and I tried not to let my face show my disappointment.

"So what's the next move?" he asked.

"A board of directors and a plan."

***

Wesley and I were able to put together a board fairly quickly. For business guidance, I had agreed to let my dad hold a spot. Ms. Corwin also eagerly joined when she heard about the project. I think she was just so happy that I had finally agreed to do the project that she was thrilled to be on the board. Nonprofit regulations required at least three board members though so we definitely needed at least one more person.

We sat in a corner of the library so that we wouldn't get shushed as often by Mrs. Champlain. We had to figure this out early before we moved on to anything else.

"What about Taylor?" I asked.

"Do you think she'd want to be on the board?"

I nodded. "It's not like she'd really have to do anything. Plus, that gets us more students involved, which can't be a bad thing."

"Do you think it matters that she isn't in the play?"

"I think it benefits us. She's an outside observer, like Ms. Corwin."

Wesley shrugged. "Works for me."

"Okay, great, then that's three. We have everyone we need, really, unless you want to add someone else."

"Three?"

I counted on my fingers. "Ms. Corwin, my dad, and Taylor, assuming she agrees. That's three."

Wesley shook his head. "Four. You forgot me."

"I didn't forget you. You're co-founder. You can't be on the board."

"I'm not co-founder."

"Wesley—"

"No, this is your thing. I never would have come up with this. You're the founder. I'm happy to be on the board. Besides, I don't want the level of work co-founder would include."

I smiled. "Fine. Then you're president of the board, and there's no arguing that."

He smirked. "Agreed."

We still hadn't talked about what had happened. For the most part, Wesley was acting like nothing had happened, but every once in a while, I got the distinct sense that he was flirting with me, though I couldn't be sure. I mean, did he have to smile at me like that, compliment me like that, *look* at me like that? It was possible that I was just reading too much into everything and that absolutely nothing was out of the ordinary, but everything was different now, and I couldn't be sure what was normal. But I did have to wonder just how long we could possibly ignore the massive elephant in the room before it crushed us.

I saw Taylor enter the library and start walking over to us, so I jumped up suddenly and shoved my stuff into my bag.

"What?" Wesley said, startled. "What just happened?"

"I just saw Taylor. I'll go talk to her about the board."

"Oh, I'll come with you." He started to get up, but I held out my hand to stop him.

"No, that's okay. I have to talk to her about our English paper, too. I'll catch up with you later."

"Uh, okay." He waved awkwardly. "Bye."

I ignored Wesley's obvious confusion and chased Taylor down. I probably could have played that cooler than I did, but what was the point?

When I caught up to Taylor, I hooked my arm around hers and practically dragged her down the hallway to the little garden where I had sat after finding out I got rejected by UF. I hadn't been there since because I didn't want to remember that moment, but it's not like I could forget that moment, so I might as well try to smother the memory with a newer, happier, but more confusing memory.

"What is your problem?" Taylor said as I slowed down. "Any particular reason you're dragging me across campus?"

"I need to talk to you."

"About?"

"Well, Wesley and I are working on this project for government, and long story short, we're starting a nonprofit to raise money to save *Beauty and the Beast* from being shut down, and we need board members, so we were thinking you'd want to be on the board, and also we kissed."

"What!" Taylor shouted and I shushed her. "What do you mean you kissed?"

"I mean we kissed. He kissed me."

"*He* kissed *you*?"

"Don't sound so surprised."

"No, no, I'm not surprised like that, I just—wow. Okay wait, when did this happen?"

"Saturday."

"And you're just now telling me about it? That was two days ago!"

"I know."

"Wait, I thought you were staying home on Saturday."

Taylor had tried to make plans with me on Saturday, but I had turned her down because I hadn't wanted to go out. I wanted to stay home and wallow and eat too much junk food without any risk of running into Sienna or Taylor or Wesley or anyone else I would have to lie to. So I told her about how Wesley had surprised me and taken me to the Strawberry Festival and how it was the most fun I'd had in a while. I told her about Barbara and Edward, about Barbara's comment, and about our conversation on the Ferris wheel.

"And then he just kissed you?"

I nodded. "I wasn't really sure he was going to do it, because why would he, but then he did."

Taylor scrunched her mouth. "How long did it last?"

"What?"

"The kiss. How long did it last?"

"I didn't clock it."

She rolled her eyes. "A few seconds, a minute?" She raised her eyebrows suggestively. "Longer?"

I smacked her arm. "I don't know, somewhere between a few seconds and a minute?"

"So are you guys a thing now?"

I threw my arms up into the air. "Who knows? That's my problem. We never really talked about it, and now he's acting pretty normal. What does that mean?"

"I don't know. I wasn't the one making out with him on a Ferris wheel."

"We were not making out."

She pointed at me. "You know I'm not going to let you live this down."

"Yeah, okay, but help me first. What do I do? Do I bring it up? Let him bring it up first?" I didn't ask the question I really needed to: *How do I tell him I didn't get into UF?*

"Well, it doesn't seem like he's going to bring it up."

"But he kissed first."

"What is this, first grade? Does it matter who was 'it'?"

I sat down on the bench and held my head in my hands. I was acutely aware that this was the same position I sat in a week ago, contemplating another seemingly impossible predicament. "Just a few days ago I was rehearsing a musical and planning for UF, and now I'm trying to figure out how to fund an entire musical and if I'm dating my best friend." *And how I'll claw my way onto UF's acceptance list.*

Taylor sat down next to me. "Do you want to be dating him?"

"I don't know," I mumbled into my hands.

"I think you do. Otherwise you wouldn't be upset that he hadn't responded yet."

I was uncomfortable with how much sense that made. "So I have to say something?"

She nodded. "It'll give you the peace of mind you need."

"Yeah, I guess."

"And maybe you'll get another kiss out of it."

"Shut up," I said, but I knew I was smiling.

"And yes," she added, "I'll be on the board. I think I heard something about that in there somewhere."

"Thanks."

She chuckled. "I can't believe y'all made out on a Ferris wheel."

"We did not make out."

"Isn't Wesley afraid of heights?"

"It wasn't the smoothest kiss, okay?"

"And yet?"

I nodded. "And yet."

10

After school, Wesley, Taylor, and I headed to Evan's Music Shop, a music store just down the street from River Glen Academy. We were hoping to convince the owner Evan to let us host some fundraisers here. If we were lucky, he might even know of some places who might be willing to donate some supplies. Evan was the kind of person who just seemed to know everyone in town, so if there was any information to be had, Evan would be the one to know it and share it.

When we arrived, Taylor immediately ditched us to head for the sheet music section. I had never been able to go to Evan's with Taylor without her walking out with at least two new pieces of sheet music. It was an addiction for sure.

"Well, if it isn't my favorite regulars," Evan said with arms spread wide.

Evan was one of those people that you just wanted to be friends with. He was super cool. He was really tall and thin with hair so straight and thin that it was reminiscent of what was likely an emo stage as a teenager, and since he was only in his twenties, perhaps the emo stage never ended. He always wore all black and would randomly play the instruments in the store whenever he felt like it. He knew how to play just about everything. Taylor had a theory that maybe he was a music prodigy, and that his parents named the store in his honor when they founded it because of his skill. I certainly wouldn't have been surprised if he was a prodigy.

"How are you, Evan?" Wesley asked.

"Hanging in there, man. What can I do for you?"

"Have you heard about River Glen's musical?"

Evan nodded. "That's a tough break. I always like to see those performances."

I added, "Well, that's actually why we're here. Wesley and I started a nonprofit business to raise money to save the musical. Mr. King has signed off on it as long as we can meet certain weekly fundraising goals. We were wondering if you'd be willing to help."

He smiled wide. "Right on. I'm always happy to help. What do you need me to do?"

"I know in the past you've hosted spirit nights where a certain portion of sales goes to the arts department. What about one that specifically benefits the musical? We also have Moe's Southwest Grill by the school hosting one this weekend."

"Nice score. Sounds great."

"And could we post some flyers?"

"For sure. We could host some kind of concert, too. I know some wicked talented musicians. I'm sure they'd be willing to help out."

"That's a fantastic idea," Wesley said.

"This is such a cool idea. Starting your own nonprofit is so creative. I'd love to be a part of something like that."

Wesley and I exchanged a glance and somehow communicated what we were both thinking. I said, "You know, we just put together a board of directors for our nonprofit, but we have an even number, and we'd prefer to have an odd number for tie breaking. Would you be interested?"

"Right on! I'd love to join."

Wesley and I high-fived each other and then Evan. This had gone perfectly. We had our fifth and final board member, new fundraising opportunities, and an update to give Mr. King that would hopefully make Mr. Quentin happy.

Wesley started hanging some flyers while he hammered out some details about the spirit night with Evan, so I drifted over to the sheet music to find Taylor.

"Evan's on board and on the board," I said.

Taylor squinted but didn't look at me. "That was too cute. So did you do it?"

"Do what?"

Taylor sighed in exasperation. "Talk to Wesley."

I looked around to make sure he wasn't listening, but he was across the store with Evan. "Taylor, I came here to talk to Evan about fundraising. You know, to save the musical and complete our very important, very time-consuming project?"

"You're stalling."

I folded my arms. "I'm not stalling. I'm prioritizing what's most important right now."

"Fine, but you're going to have to deal with it eventually."

"I know."

***

It felt pretty weird being at Moe's without being behind the counter in a neon green shirt that smelled like queso. I was surprised I had even talked my boss Gina into it. Usually she was pretty opposed to fundraisers, but I guilt tripped her pretty hard over how she should care about the arts, and she caved. It didn't hurt that her ten-year-old daughter who had just been dropped off from ballet rehearsal overheard the conversation and begged her mom to help us out.

Gina let me commandeer a table to decorate with information about the school, the musical, and donation buckets. The night was still young, and the fundraiser had only started about twenty minutes ago, but I was already nervous about the lack of customers. Not only did we need a lot more people in the door to raise enough money, but Gina would be furious if she had any cause to suggest that this event had hurt business even if it hadn't.

"Hey," Rachel said as she walked in. "How's it going so far?"

I shrugged. "Could be better, but it's still early I guess. You look really cute."

Rachel held out the edges of her yellow dress. "Thanks. Maybe it sounds kind of silly, but I thought I'd dress the part, you know?"

"It's not silly. It's a good idea. Maybe we should have covered Drew in fake fur."

Rachel laughed louder than I had ever heard her laugh before. "That would have been hilarious. He's coming by later. You should suggest that to him, but I want to be there when you do to see his face."

"Definitely."

"You look great too, by the way. I love that shirt."

"Thanks. It's weird not wearing a Moe's uniform," I said, but that wasn't the only reason it was weird. I wore this shirt because Wesley once complimented it at Taylor's birthday party last year. It's the only time I can remember him complimenting my appearance before the Strawberry Festival. I didn't normally wear it because it was floral patterned and just a little too frilly for me, but he had liked it.

"I bet. Well, I'll see you later. Let me know if I can help!"

A few more people came in behind Rachel, and her parents donated a decent amount, but we still weren't gaining enough traction. We still had two hours to go. I had to hope people would come through. Most of the cast arrived within the first half hour, but they weren't exactly the ones bringing in the cash.

Every time I heard my coworkers shout a chorus of "Welcome to Moe's"—and I fought the urge to say it, too—I looked at the door to see who had arrived and how many of them there were. I'd seen a lot of our cast members show up with their families, but for some stupid reason, I wasn't ready to see Wesley walk in.

Of course I knew he was coming. He had a lead role. He was my project partner. I'd worn this stupid shirt for him after all. But maybe I just hadn't expected to feel that tightness in my chest when he walked in. Maybe I hadn't expected to notice how good he looked in a black polo and dark-wash jeans. I definitely hadn't expected to smell the same cologne I smelled on him that night on the Ferris wheel while our lips were touching.

"Hey," Wesley said with a smile. "Good turnout so far?"

I attempted to shrug. "Not what I was hoping for."

"There's still time." He picked up the donation bucket and shook it. "This seems promising."

"Mostly ones and fives. Not as promising as it seems."

He set the bucket down and nodded. There was a moment of awkward silence before he said, "You look nice. I mean you always look nice—I mean—usually when I see you here, you're dressed like a highlighter."

"Gee, thanks."

He shoved his hands in his pockets. "You know what I mean. Those Moe's shirts—"

"Yeah, they're pretty electric."

He nodded again, and it seemed like he was about to say something when Drew's little sister started squealing cheerfully.

"Please," she said. "Pretty please for me?"

Drew said to her, "Not right now, Abby."

"Pleeeeeaaase?" she said louder. She had folded her hands and was giving him her best puppy dog eyes.

"What does she want?" Wesley asked.

Drew rolled his eyes. "She's trying to convince me to sing something from the musical. She does this all the time at home. Seems to be no convincing her that I can't right now."

"I mean," Wesley said, "if your public demands it."

Drew hesitated while Abby continued begging. He really seemed to be struggling with the decision of randomly bursting into song in the middle of a restaurant, but Abby was incessant. Finally, he held out his hand to Rachel. "Only if my leading lady will join me."

Rachel blushed but took his hand, and Drew immediately burst into singing the title song "Beauty and the Beast." Rachel and Drew had such natural chemistry that they really were dynamite to watch perform together. We hadn't gotten very far in rehearsals before Mr. King had shut it down, but I could really see now why they were cast opposite each other. It wasn't just that they were each good at their own part: they sold their romance so successfully. I knew Rachel liked Drew, but watching them now, the way Drew looked at Rachel, I was pretty sure it was mutual.

At first, I was a little worried that this impromptu performance would annoy the customers, but quite to the contrary, they were really enjoying it. Some were filming, most were applauding, and increasingly larger numbers of people were asking who they were and why they were performing. I started circulating with the bucket and telling people as I went around why there were teenagers randomly singing at Moe's on a Thursday night, and donations started flooding in. This was making a huge difference, and all because of Drew's persistent little sister.

When Drew and Rachel finished, after a hearty applause, clamoring started for a performance from Gaston. Wesley laughed, grabbed a hold of Jamar, who played LeFou, jumped onto a tabletop, and started belting "Gaston" in his best, goofiest Gaston voice. Wesley was pretty much the only person who was surprised by his casting as Gaston. He was so perfect for the role. He was so good at putting on all the bravado of Gaston while still being charming and, of course, good-looking. He moved just the right way, winked at Rachel in a way that made the customers smile, and when he propped his arm up on Jamar's head while singing, everyone roared with laughter. Rachel played off of him perfectly, too, but Rachel and Drew were definitely in danger of Wesley stealing the show with humor.

The song ended with the perfect eye roll from Rachel, and the customers erupted into applause. The restaurant was nearly full at this point. The performances must have attracted attention from passers-by. The bucket I had been passing around was full of bills. I couldn't be sure how much money it was until I counted it, but it was certainly better than I had anticipated based on the way the night started out.

Rachel was singing "Home" now and moving everyone who could hear her. She was spectacular, and wearing that yellow dress, she was undeniably Belle. I snuck a glance at Drew and found him riveted by her.

Wesley flopped into the chair next to me, sweaty from his exuberant performance, and propped up his arm on the chair back.

"So?" he asked.

"So what?"

"How was I? Spectacular?"

I laughed. "Still in the spirit of Gaston, I see."

"This is fun. Reminds me of why I want to save the musical."

"Had you forgotten?"

He shrugged. "I don't know. I guess maybe I just got so focused on winning the competition and setting up the business with you that I forgot why we were doing it."

"I know what you mean." Sometimes I wondered if I was really doing this for the musical. If we saved the musical but I didn't get off the waitlist at UF, would I think it was worth it?

***

"$320. You?"

I sighed. "$448."

Once the night was over, Wesley and I stayed behind at Moe's to count all the money. It had seemed like a lot in the bucket, but there were so many ones and fives, that it hadn't amounted to as much as I initially thought it would.

"That's not bad," Wesley said.

"Yeah, but it's not good. We're supposed to give Mr. King one grand on Monday. We didn't even break $800."

"But we still have our deal with Evan and the concert this weekend. Plus the bake sale tomorrow. It could still happen."

"It's not coming in fast enough. At this rate, we'll never raise ten grand in time."

What had I gotten myself into? For some stupid reason, I thought this would be easier than it had been. So far, it's been nothing but mediocrity.

"Have faith."

"Wesley, this isn't working. What are we going to do?"

"Fix it."

I flopped back in my chair. "Because it's just that easy."

"No, because that's the only solution. We need to fix it, at least short-term to convince Mr. Quentin. Evan's concert is on Saturday. What can we do before then? Anything?"

I shook my head. "We wouldn't be able to throw something together that fast. At least, not something people would actually attend on short notice."

"What about at the concert?"

I thought about how the night had gone. We hadn't had many customers, and even as time went on and more people came in, the donations were not flowing. We got the majority of our $800 during the impromptu performances. Maybe that was the answer.

"What if we performed at the concert?"

"You and me?"

"The cast. Like you guys did tonight. That caught everyone's attention."

Wesley nodded. "It's a good idea. Would we just sing *Beauty and the Beast* songs again?"

"Maybe. Or maybe sing random stuff. If people see what kind of talent is involved in the musical, they might be more willing to donate."

"Are you sure?" he asked. "I don't know, it's one thing to have people drop some spare change at a fast food joint. I'm not so sure that it would bring in real money."

"Why not? It's basically a concert without charging admission."

"I guess it could work. We should definitely get Rachel and Drew to do a duet regardless of what they sing. They were so good together."

"Definitely."

"Speaking of, did you know that Drew asked Rachel to prom?"

I gasped. "He did? That's adorable."

"Yeah. He asked her a couple of days ago."

"I can't believe she didn't tell me. We were talking earlier tonight."

"I don't think they've really told people. Drew asked me like a week ago if he should ask her publicly or privately."

I smacked his arm, and he ducked and laughed. "You've known for a week and didn't tell me? Rude."

"I didn't want to say anything until he actually asked. You know, in case he chickened out."

"But I'm your best friend. When you know stuff, you are automatically obligated to tell me." I felt a pang in my chest as soon as I had said those words. Wesley wasn't the one lying to his best friend.

He smirked. "Fine, then I guess I'm obligated to tell you this: Drew is renting a limo for prom. He asked if I wanted to get in on that."

"You're going to third wheel Drew and Rachel?"

He rolled his eyes. "No, I'm not that weird. How about you come with me?"

Wait, did he just— "What?"

He slid a small plastic box of chocolate covered strawberries over to me that he had pulled from his backpack. "Would you like to go to prom with me?"

I looked down at the strawberries. They were covered in white chocolate. He knew I liked that better than milk or dark chocolate. "Uh, yeah. Yes."

"Yes?"

I nodded, trying to sound more emphatic and less confused. "Yes. Sounds like fun."

"Great. I'll let Drew know we're in."

"Are we splitting cost? Because I can—"

"Nope, not a chance. I've got this. Goodnight, Jorie."

"Goodnight."

Wesley just asked me to prom?

11

— · —

I had actually sunk so low that I had resorted to bake sales.

When I had decided to do a massive project that involved a lot of fundraising, I really hadn't wanted to do a bake sale. Bake sales were unoriginal, boring, a lot of work, and not a lot of profit. How was a bake sale supposed to win a competition? How was a bake sale supposed to get me admission to UF? It was a terrible idea.

But the musical fundraising efforts were struggling, and we had to do everything we possibly could. If a bake sale could help at all, it was worth it. Wesley kept trying to remind me that a bake sale was a good idea regardless, and that variety in events would probably look good, and that any money coming in was good, and maybe all of that was true, but I was still a little ticked. Was resorting to something this basic just a symptom of failure?

Ms. Corwin had given us the authorization to set up a table in the courtyard before school, during lunch, and after school. Over the weekend I contacted the cast, and I'd managed to get a lot of the cast members to contribute something, which was nice since it saved me hours of baking. I just talked my mom into making some mini pies, and everyone else filled in the gaps. I had to admit that everything looked delicious. Rachel brought cupcakes, Wesley rice cereal treats, Drew chocolate chip cookies, Jamar blondies, Devon brownies, Caroline sugar cookies, Laura whoopie pies, Elizabeth homemade candy, and Tiffany banana bread. Pretty much the only high schooler that hadn't participated was Sienna, as expected. She had, however, made a show of asking which item Rachel had contributed.

I pointed at the devil's food cupcakes. "She made those."

Sienna scrunched her nose. "Looks a little like dog food, don't you think?"

Drew shot her a dirty look, picked up five cupcakes, handed me a ten dollar bill, and scarfed one in front of her before handing the others to his friends who similarly shoved them in their faces. Sienna stormed off in a huff, and I gave them a wink.

"Hey," Taylor said, dumping her backpack under the table. "Sorry I'm late."

"It's fine."

"Wow, this is a lot of stuff."

I nodded. "And I've already sold, like, a fourth of it. People contributed a ton."

"That's fantastic."

I shrugged. "Everything costs two dollars. It's not exactly lucrative."

"Every dollar counts, right?"

"That's what Wesley says."

"And you don't agree?"

I huffed. "Bake sales just aren't really my jam here. I feel like I'm wasting time, but I'm here, so I'm going to sell absolutely everything on this table."

"Geez, tense."

"Sorry," I muttered.

"What's your deal?"

"Last night didn't bring in nearly as much as I had hoped. The entire thing is falling apart."

Taylor didn't say anything right away since a parent was buying some cookies. Once he walked away, she tapped my arm so I would make eye contact with her.

"If this is meant to be, it will be. You just have to trust that."

"Trust doesn't mean anything. I have to make it happen."

"And I believe you can do that, but I also believe that you're getting a little crazy. You've got to relax. Did you talk to Wesley?"

"Yeah."

"And?"

"He asked me to prom."

"That's great."

"Oh, sure, I'm just gonna go to prom with Wesley, who I may or may not be dating, pretending that everything is normal, acting like my entire life isn't falling apart and like if I fail at this project, not only will I not get into UF, but I'll disappoint the entire school. It's been a fantastic week, it really has."

Taylor grabbed my arm, practically dragged me out of my chair, and asked Rachel to cover the table for a minute. She pulled me around the corner into the restroom where, thankfully, there was no one. She locked the door behind us and turned to face me.

"Talk."

"About what?"

"You're obviously upset about everything. What happened with UF?"

In my meltdown, I hadn't even realized that I'd said something about UF. I was trying, in vain, to recall my exact words. How much had I said? Who had heard besides Taylor?

"Right now? We're supposed to be bake saling."

"I don't think that's a verb, and Rachel is more than capable of selling for a little while. If anything, she might sell more than us with that Disney princess vibe she's got going on. Now, come on. Out with it."

I folded my arms. "I didn't get into UF."

"But I thought—"

"I lied, okay? I lied. Sienna was bragging, and I was really upset, and I panicked."

Telling Taylor simultaneously felt right and wrong. It was somewhat of a relief to let it out to *someone*, but the more people that knew, the worse I felt about lying to Wesley, my parents, Ms. Corwin, and everyone else.

To my surprise, though I expected Taylor to be mad or annoyed that I lied to her, her arms dropped to her side, and she looked sad for me. It was almost worse. "Oh my gosh. I knew something was wrong that day, but I didn't think—I can't believe they rejected you."

"They didn't really." I explained everything about the waitlist and the project and how I hadn't told anyone except for Savannah.

"Why, Jorie? Why didn't you say anything?"

"I was too embarrassed. UF is all I've talked about for years. I couldn't take the embarrassment, and now it's been too long to come clean."

"But why haven't you talked to Wesley?"

I shrugged. "Haven't had a chance. We've been so busy with the project. I had planned to bring it up a few days ago, but then the kiss happened, and everything got weird, and then he asked me to prom."

"What's the end game here?"

"What do you mean?"

"Are you trying to get with Wesley or win the competition?"

"So I can't do both?"

"Of course you can, but not without being honest with Wesley. He thinks you're doing this for him."

I hesitated. "He does?"

She nodded. "He was telling me just the other day how he thinks it's so cool that you're working so hard on this thing for the sake of the musical and for him. Because he asked you to."

"Why does that matter?" I asked, as if I didn't know. My worst fears were true. Wesley thought I was this incredibly selfless person who was acting out of concern for the school and for him when I was doing neither, really. Sure, I cared about Wesley, and sure, I wanted the musical to happen, but that wasn't the real reason I was having a meltdown in the bathroom during a bake sale.

"You know if you told him the truth that he would help you, but if you don't tell him, and he finds out, he's going to be hurt."

"I don't think so," I said, but some part of me knew that she was right. Wesley would be mad about the lie. But isn't it too late for that now? Isn't the lie too deep? "I just can't tell him."

She held up her hands in surrender. "Fine, but don't say I didn't warn you." She unlocked the bathroom door. "Coming?"

"In a sec."

I didn't like thinking about what Wesley would do or say or even think if I was honest with him. It felt like it was too late to say anything now. No matter what, he'd be mad. Besides, did I really owe him anything? Was it really so bad that I had my own reasons for doing the project? Hadn't Ms. Corwin tried to bribe us into participating by offering extra credit, and wasn't Dale Henchard offering prize money as incentive? There was nothing wrong with wanting something and doing whatever it took to achieve it.

I washed my hands, flicked some cool water on my face and dried it, and walked out of the bathroom straight into Mrs. Gonzalez. Her daughter Maria Gonzalez had graduated last year. She and I were pretty friendly last year when we both took Italian together.

"Sorry, Mrs. Gonzalez. I wasn't looking."

She laughed. "That's okay, Marjorie. How are you?"

I forced a smile. "All right. How's Maria? She's at Auburn University, right?"

"She is," she said with a wide, proud smile. "She's loving it. I'll tell her I ran into you. I just stopped by to bring Julianna lunch." Julianna was Maria's little sister. I was pretty sure she was a freshman. "So, what's this going on outside?"

"Oh, we're doing a bake sale. We're trying to raise money to save the musical."

"Save it?"

I explained the whole thing to Mrs. Gonzalez, and she listened intently, looking genuinely upset.

"You know, I always tried to get Maria to participate in those, but she just didn't like them. I did theater in high school and college, you know."

"That's really cool."

"I always loved it. I'm so sorry to hear that you've lost so many sponsors."

"It's been rough. I'm trying to raise enough money to give the sponsors confidence that their money won't be wasted, but it's hard."

She had her arms crossed, and her finger started tapping her crossed arm. "Can I help in any way?"

I laughed. "Buy a brownie?"

"I was thinking something a little bigger. I'd be happy to contribute, especially if it can help you get some other sponsors."

Parents. Alumni. Dang it, why hadn't I thought of that before? That was such an obvious solution to the problem. A lot of parents would probably turn us down since they pay tuition and all, but who knew? Some parents might be willing to contribute. Besides, we call alumni for donations for athletics. Why couldn't we do the same for the arts? Former theater kids with any kind of money would probably be willing to donate.

"Really? That would be incredible."

"Unfortunately, I don't have my checkbook with me. Can I bring it by later?"

"Actually, we're having a concert at Evan's Music Shop on Saturday night. You could bring it then."

"Perfect." She smiled. "See you then."

After she walked away, I realized that she hadn't said a number, so I had no idea if she was offering $100, $500, or $2000. I supposed any amount was worthwhile, but I was definitely hoping it would be a substantial amount. Maybe after that, the bake sale, the spirit night, and the concert, things would finally turn around a little bit.

"Hey," Wesley said, turning the corner. "I was just coming over to find you at the bake sale."

"On my way there now."

"So I feel a little bad that you're doing all the work."

"Those are the terms we agreed to."

Wesley rolled his eyes. "Don't sound so formal. I'm just saying I could take some of the work to make it more equal."

"I'm fine."

Of course, I wasn't fine, but I had no idea how to communicate that to Wesley. Taylor was right: I needed to be honest with him. He was being so nice, so supportive, that I couldn't keep lying to him anymore. He should know the real reason I was so invested in this. He would still help. Right?

"I mean, if we're going to get this thing off the ground, you might need me to help."

I stopped walking. "You think we can't do it with things as they are now?"

"I didn't say that."

"Do you think I can't do this?"

He sighed. "Jorie, you know I didn't say that. I just want to be sure that we're both doing everything we can. I think you might be underestimating what a big project this is."

He didn't believe in us? He didn't think we could pull this off?

"I'm not underestimating anything. It'll be fine. *I'll* be fine. Everything is going to work out."

But what if it didn't? What if Mr. Quentin shut the whole thing down before I could fix it? What if I couldn't fix it even if Mr. Quentin didn't shut it down? What if this whole thing was destined to fail?

***

I had tried to avoid this meeting at all costs, but it seemed impossible. Mr. Quentin decided that he wanted to meet with the board of Spotlight Heroes to make sure we were on track, and of course, we weren't. I was at least grateful for the presence of the other board members so that it wasn't just Mr. Quentin staring Wesley and me down.

The thing was that Mr. Quentin wasn't a bad guy. He was actually a really good principal. He just had a natural talent for being intimidating when he wasn't trying. He was very tall, and I think that added to his imposing presence. He was older, and he did that thing that older people usually did where they would look over their glasses at you instead of taking them off. I didn't know why it was always so creepy when people did that.

Sitting in that room, I could have laughed looking at the board. It was certainly eclectic, and it probably wouldn't make much sense to Mr. Quentin. Before him sat three high school students, a dad, a young and cool teacher, and a kind of emo music shop owner. That didn't even account for Mr. King sitting in the corner with a scarf patterned like *Starry, Starry Night*. The bunch of us certainly didn't look like a professional board of a nonprofit organization except for my dad and maybe Ms. Corwin.

Mr. Quentin sat down and tried not to notice Evan's feet propped up on the edge of the table. "Thank you all for sitting down with me. Your time is appreciated. I wanted to have a discussion about this endeavor to fund the school musical. Mr. King tells me he approved this provided certain fundraising goals could be met."

"Indeed, sir," Mr. King said. "I thought Miss Haywood and Mr. Dixon deserved the right to try. I'm quite proud of their tenacity."

"Ms. Corwin, does this endeavor meet the requirements of the project you are sponsoring?"

"Yes," Ms. Corwin said. "It's a wonderfully creative project. I think they've got a shot at winning."

He nodded a short nod. "I know Miss Haywood and Mr. Dixon to be very studious, determined, and creative young people, but I must say that I am concerned about the outlook of this endeavor." Why did he keep calling it an "endeavor"? It sounded creepy. "Mr. King has worked very hard to fund this musical and has thus far been unsuccessful. I'm unwilling to allow this to continue if it will ultimately fail."

"It won't fail," I said suddenly and a little too loudly. "Sir, it won't fail. I'm not willing to let it fail."

"I believe you, Miss Haywood, but Mr. King's budget is high, and I don't know if this is attainable this quickly. Perhaps for next year it would be possible, but it seems like too big of a mountain at this time."

Was he trying to shut us down? "Mr. King said that he had other sponsors who dropped out when Mr. Bunton dropped out, assuming the musical was canceled. If we can show them that some of the funds are coming through, I think they'll reconsider their decision."

He tilted his head. He seemed to be considering that. "That's a reasonable argument, but I'm still hesitant. What do you have thus far?"

I swallowed hard. I had hoped to have more money raised at this point. Mr. Quentin wouldn't be impressed by the lack of profit from the Moe's spirit night and bake sale. "Just over two thousand, sir. The rights have already been paid for by Mr. King, and that was about one thousand."

His eyes widened slowly. "So you've only raised about one thousand?"

"Yes, but I talked to a former River Glen parent this morning who said she was willing to contribute."

"How much?"

"She didn't say. She's bringing a check to the concert this weekend."

Mr. Quentin sighed.

"Sir, if I may," my dad said, "I've helped start many nonprofits in my line of work, and they all start slowly. I have yet to see a nonprofit start immediately with high funds. It takes time for them to get going."

I added, "Plus, we have more events planned for this weekend. We think those will make a big difference."

Mr. Quentin nodded again. He was like a lethargic bobblehead. "Mr. Haywood, you feel confident in your daughter's attempts?"

"I do."

"Ms. Corwin and Mr. King, do you think this has the potential to succeed?" They both agreed. "Mr. Green, what are your thoughts?"

Evan kicked his feet off the desk and sat up. "I'm always down to support the arts, man."

I had to suppress the laughter I felt rising in my throat at the look on Mr. Quentin's face. I risked a glance at Wesley and saw a vein popping out of his neck, and I knew that he was holding back his own amusement. I wondered why he hadn't said anything. Was he trying not to infringe on me, or was he secretly siding with Mr. Quentin?

"Here's what I can do. I'm willing to see what you all can do. Continue with your events this weekend as planned, and we will reconvene on Monday to check your progress."

"Thank you, Mr. Quentin," I said.

"But I must be straightforward with you. If you have not made significant progress after this weekend, I will have to move forward with the shutting down of the musical. Understood?"

I forced myself to smile to avoid looking panicked. "Understood."

We walked out of the board meeting, said goodbye to everyone, and Wesley tugged my arm to lead me around the corner. He looked around to make sure no one was listening and crossed his arms.

"Are you insane?" he asked.

"What do you mean?"

"We have no guarantee that the concert will do any better than the spirit night at Moe's."

"No, we don't, but we don't have any guarantee that it'll fail either."

He rubbed his face and huffed. "Jorie, we're in way over our heads."

"We are not."

"Mr. Quentin thinks we're some reckless, irresponsible kids or something."

I rolled my eyes. "He does not. He just wants to see tangible progress."

"Which we don't have."

"Which we *will* have. Why are you freaking out on me?"

"Jorie, you promised that we wouldn't keep pushing it. You said that if we couldn't make it work, we'd throw in the towel before it got out of hand."

"Yeah?"

He gestured his arms wildly. "Well, it's getting out of hand."

I sat down on a bench. "Just have a little faith."

He numbered out his complaints on his fingers. "We don't have enough money. Mr. Quentin and Mr. King think we're going to fail. We don't have enough time to do this. We have no guarantees that anything we try will work. We have one good fundraising idea, and it probably won't bring in ten grand."

"Eight grand."

"What?"

"We already have two grand."

He sighed. "You know what I mean. This is reckless."

"What happened to all of your optimism at the bake sale? You were so sure it would work then."

"I hoped it would, but that was before Mr. Quentin doubted us."

I stood up again and folded my arms. "Is this why you didn't say anything that whole meeting? You were so chatty when we met with Mr. King, and then suddenly you become silent."

"I didn't want to lie to Mr. Quentin."

"I didn't lie to Mr. Quentin." I might have been lying to myself and to everyone else, but that was a separate issue altogether.

"This is out of control. You heard Mr. King the other day. The disappointment is going to be magnified if we fail at this."

"Ugh, we're *not* going to fail. Why does everyone keep saying that?"

"Because it's a real possibility!"

I knew that. Of course I knew that. I knew that the chances of this failing were extraordinarily high, but I was unwilling to admit that to myself, much less to anyone else. This whole thing felt like it hinged on Wesley not giving up on me, and now he seemed to be doing just that. I really needed him to buy into this.

I put a hand on each of Wesley's shoulders. "Do you really want to give up on the musical?"

"No, but—"

"Then let's not give up."

He sighed, and his eyes rolled faster than I thought it was possible for eyes to roll. "Fine, but if Mr. Quentin ends up having to shut us down, it's going to look bad for us, your dad, Mr. King, Ms. Corwin, Mr. Quentin, everyone. We're going to be hated."

"Then we do whatever it takes to convince Mr. Quentin not to shut us down."

Wesley stared at me for a moment, just for a moment, and then backed away slowly. Did we just have a fight? Were fights different now? I couldn't tell.

I was losing supporters for my plans the more time that went by. I had kind of thought Wesley was a guarantee, someone that would always be on my side, but he was frustrated with me, and I didn't know how to fix it. Every time something like this came up, I thought about just telling him the truth, the real reason I was fighting so hard to make this work, but I just couldn't do it. Would he still want to do this if he knew the real reason wasn't for *Beauty and the Beast*? Would he think I was a bad friend for not telling him sooner? Would he think I was selfish for doing whatever it took to make UF happen? Taylor had more than implied that Wesley would be upset if I didn't tell him, but I wasn't ready to find out the answers to any of those questions.

What I did know is that if I had any chance at all of making this happen, I needed Wesley's help, so losing his support was not an option. I had to win him over again.

"Hey," I said. "I was thinking of swinging by the music shop after school tomorrow. We still need to hammer out a few details with Evan. Maybe he'll have some good ideas of stuff we can add that will help.'

He shrugged lazily. "Worth a shot, I guess."

"Will you come with me?"

He seemed surprised. Was he not my project partner? "Sure, if you want."

"Of course. We are partners, after all. Besides, you are better at planning that kind of stuff anyway."

He snorted. "I think Evan's got a handle on that, don't you?"

"Yeah, but I still want your help. Are you in?"

"I'm in."

I couldn't be sure exactly what Wesley was thinking, but at least I had talked him off the proverbial ledge and gotten him to continue with this project. I had known that this project would be hard, but I had only really considered the challenges of the project itself. I never gave any thought to the people involved. This whole thing was becoming more emotional than I had anticipated. I had to hope that it would pay off and that it would all be worth it in the end.

12

— · —

"Cut! Everyone freeze," Mr. King shouted, and when the house lights came up, I could see that he was gesticulating wildly. This was at least the tenth time he'd interrupted today's rehearsal. At this rate, we were never going to get through this scene.

"We have to start that song over," he said with a dramatic sigh. "That choreography was sloppy. Wesley and Jamar, you two have got to be extraordinary."

Wesley huffed a little. "But Mr. King, we've done this song like fifteen times. Does it have to be extraordinary at every rehearsal?"

Mr. King gripped his heart like he'd been shot. "Mr. Dixon, this song is called 'Gaston' for a reason. If Gaston himself is not perfect every time, who else will be?"

Wesley knew better than to argue at that point, so he just nodded, and Mr. King gestured for the music to start over. The track clicked on, and the lights came down again. Technically, I was in this scene, but since Mr. King was determined to get Gaston and LeFou's choreography right, he'd let everyone that didn't dance in this scene sit down, and thankfully, that included me for the time being. For a little while, I got to just watch the rehearsal.

I always knew that Wesley could sing, but I guess I had never really paid close attention to it before now. He was really good. If he hadn't been so perfect for Gaston, he might've been able to make a play for the role of the Beast. I couldn't count the number of productions I'd watched Wesley in, but it was like I was watching him for the first time now. Every time he smiled out at the audience, elbowed Jamar, or flexed while standing on a table, I couldn't ignore the flutter I felt in my chest.

But everything was still so up in the air. Yeah, he'd asked me to prom, but did that really mean anything? I just felt like I couldn't be sure, but I also couldn't deny that I really enjoyed watching him perform. It was becoming more and more apparent that I had feelings I was hoping he reciprocated.

"Cut!"

Everyone groaned. The lights came up again, and Mr. King rubbed his temples. "Let's rewind a little bit. I feel like we've lost our flow. Let's go back a scene or two to the castle. I need all the furniture, Belle, and the Beast. Let's run the dialogue before Belle's solo and maybe by the time we transition to 'Gaston,' it will run better."

Sienna grunted and pushed herself out of her chair. "What's the point of this, anyway?"

Caroline smirked. "Mr. King wants his flow."

"No, I mean rehearsals. Why are we practicing for a show that's going to get shut down *again*?"

It felt like a punch to the gut. No one had been willing to say it out loud until now, until Sienna, but everyone was thinking it. Rehearsals weren't running well, and it was because no one was sure it was really going to happen. Why put in all the energy if it was doomed in the end?

"Come on," Caroline said, waving at Sienna to go to the stage, "if we don't get up there, Mr. King is going to lose it."

She smiled at me as she passed, and I returned the smile as a thanks, but it wasn't lost on me that Caroline hadn't argued with Sienna. No one was confident in this, and that included Wesley. That even included me.

I needed to do something big, something tangible to reassure everyone. If I could pull in enough money with the concert or from alumni like Mrs. Gonzalez, maybe I could restore some faith in this musical. Maybe the rest of the cast would finally start to believe that it was possible. Maybe I could convince them to believe in me, to trust in me.

And maybe, just maybe, I could start to believe in myself.

***

Wesley and I spent hours after school at Evan's the next day planning the concert on Saturday. Evan had a few friends planning to perform, and we had managed to talk him into performing as well, but we were really hoping this new idea of having the cast perform would draw in more people, thereby bringing in more donations. It wasn't the craziest idea, but we also had no idea if it would work, and even if it did, the spare change we brought in at Moe's wasn't enough. We needed people to be willing to make substantial donations based on the performances of a few high school kids.

"Hey, I was thinking," I said, "about some ways we might be able to bring in more money. Mrs. Gonzalez gave me the idea. What if we contacted alumni or parents who used to have kids at River Glen? They might donate."

"You think?" Wesley asked.

I shrugged. "Why not? It can't hurt, right? The worst they can do is say no."

"That's an awkward phone conversation if they do."

"Yeah, maybe, but what if they say yes? Mrs. Gonzalez was willing to donate just like that. I'm sure others would, too."

Evan folded his arms and leaned back. "It's a good idea. I have such good memories of being on that stage."

Wesley said, "I always forget that you graduated from River Glen Academy."

"Yeah. Some of the best years of my life. If I had the money, I'd donate."

"Letting us host a concert here is more than enough," I said. "But thank you."

The phone rang, and Evan glanced over. "Sorry, I have to take that."

Evan had stepped out for a few minutes to talk to someone, so Wesley and I were left alone in the music shop with nothing to do except stare at a wall of guitars that neither of us knew how to play.

After an awkward pause, Wesley asked, "So how are we going to get a list of names?"

"I figure we ask Mr. King. I'm sure he has their information."

Wesley nodded in agreement but didn't say anything.

I still didn't know where we stood. We'd kissed. It had been great, and we'd never discussed it. Now we were going to prom together, and I didn't know what that meant. It wouldn't be the first time: we'd gone to homecoming together sophomore year. We both really didn't want to go without dates, so we'd agreed to go together strictly as friends, and we'd had the best time. I certainly had more fun with him than when I went with Sean Hayden junior year. Worst five month relationship of my life. There was no doubt that if Wesley and I went to prom together, we'd have a good time. But was that all it was? He hadn't defined it as friends like he did last time, but then, he hadn't exactly defined it as a date either. Although, if chocolate covered strawberries didn't scream "date," then I didn't know what did.

Suddenly, Wesley asked, "Do you have the list of everyone who's signed up to perform?"

"Yeah." I handed him the list.

All of the students cast in major roles had signed up along with a few others. We had even convinced a few people to perform more than once: Drew and Rachel were performing together but also each doing a solo. Sienna was singing twice, unfortunately, but we'd also convinced Rafael to sing twice since he'd planned to sing "Be Our Guest" as Lumiere, but he had a spectacular voice even when he was not playing a French candlestick. Combined with the performers Evan was bringing who were sure to be top notch, this was shaping up to be really impressive.

Wesley looked up from the list with a puzzled expression. "You're not on here."

"And?"

"You're not performing?"

I shook my head. "Not a lead."

"Neither are Jamar or Tiffany or Monique, but they're signed up."

I pointed a finger. "They can sing."

"Who says you can't?"

"Savannah. Especially when I wake her up in the morning in the shower."

He couldn't help but laugh. "Fine, but you have a singing role because you can sing."

"I have a singing role because there are only three sopranos who can stay on key and one of them is Rachel."

He waved the list in front of me. "You know you want to."

"I definitely don't."

"Fine, but the people who come tonight won't know what they're missing."

"Oh, because you've heard me sing?"

"Yeah, I hear you're one of only three sopranos who can stay on key."

I shoved him by the arm. "Shut up."

"Besides, I've been in the car with you while you belt out some Taylor Swift. You've got skills."

"Whatever."

Evan walked in with a big smile. "Good news, guys. Alfredo next door says he wants in on the event."

Alfredo owned the coffee shop next door. He was that classic grandfatherly type who just made you smile to be around. He was so sweet, and he'd owned that coffee shop since my parents were in high school.

"What do you mean?" Wesley asked.

"Walk with me."

We followed Evan out back behind the coffee shop. He had a little stage set up out there with lights strung over it and around the entire backyard area. He had a small stage inside for smaller performances, but he used the outside stage for bigger events. It was encouraging that he was planning for our event to be big. He already had a bunch of tables set up, and his cousin Rhett who worked there part-time was setting up more.

Evan said, "I was thinking that if we served food and beverages, we could bring probably do better business, but that's definitely not my forte. I asked Alfredo if he'd be willing to help out."

"So he's serving drinks?" I asked.

Evan nodded. "Coffee, tea, soda, water, and he's even offering some of his pastries at a slightly inflated rate. He says he wants the difference to go to Spotlight Heroes."

"That's incredible," Wesley said.

I said to Wesley, "We'll have to go by after this and thank him."

"He's really excited to see all the performances," Evan said. "I think he secretly offered to help so he can hang out and watch."

"He could've done that anyway," I said. "But this is huge. This could double our profits."

"Easily."

Evan walked us through everything else he had planned, and I gave him the schedule of performers with blank slots alloted for him and his friends. We set up a few collection buckets in the music shop, coffee shop, and a few outside as well. Wesley had the great idea to put a little bucket on each table to encourage donations as people perform without people having to get up, so we put a few coin jars out as well. This was our Hail Mary: if this didn't bring in substantial cash, then we had no hope of raising a total of ten grand. I was sure this would put us over our first goal, but we needed a lot more than that. This was going to work. It *had* to, especially if I was going to have any leveraging power to get UF to take a second look at me.

After working everything out with Evan, we went next door and thanked Alfredo for his help, then headed over to my truck. Wesley's car was getting worse, and he didn't want to put any more strain on it than he had to, so I'd driven him to school today. Up until now, he had been pretty chill about whether or not we won the competition, but now that the prize money seemed to be his only way to fix up his car quickly, he was just as anxious as I was to win.

"So," he said, rubbing the back of his neck, "any chance I can persuade you to pick me up again tomorrow night?"

"Of course."

"I appreciate it. It's really shaking a lot."

"Are you going to be able to drive to school on Monday?"

He shrugged. "Hope so. If not, you might be getting a 6am phone call."

I laughed. "As if you've ever woken up at 6am for school."

"Fair enough."

"So what time do you want me to pick you up tomorrow? I'm thinking we should get there early. What do you think, like half an hour early?"

We hopped into the truck, and Wesley nodded. "That sounds good. Hey, I was thinking. As good as Alfredo's stuff is, I don't really want to survive the whole night on coffee and croissants. What do you think about getting dinner beforehand?"

"Sure," I said without thinking and then wondered if I had just accepted a date invitation. "Where were you thinking?"

"It's a surprise."

"How is it a surprise if I'm driving?"

"I have my ways."

13

"Savannah," I called from my closet. "Come here."

"Why?" she yelled.

"Just come here."

Our bedrooms shared a wall, so we'd always been able to hear each other through the wall. My closet wall was right next to her desk. When we were in middle school, I used to sit in the closet in blast music, and it drove her insane.

Savannah walked in. "What do you want?"

"Help me pick a dress."

"I thought you were wearing the pink one."

"Well, I'm not sure now."

"Why?"

"Just because."

"But why though? You don't usually stress these things. You're such a planner that you always pick your outfits like days in advance."

I huffed. I had to do it. "I think I'm dating Wesley."

Her eyes widened. "What do you mean you 'think'? Either you are or you aren't."

"He asked me to prom."

"So?"

"And he asked me to dinner before the concert."

"You guys do that literally all of the time."

"Not since we kissed."

"You kissed?"

"At the Strawberry Festival. On the Ferris wheel."

"The Ferris wheel? Oh, Jorie, how cliché."

I dismissed her with a flick of my hand. "Yeah, I know."

She squinted and pointed a finger at me. "I knew something was up with you two."

I rolled my eyes. "You thought we were fighting."

Savannah closed her eyes and waved her arms a little. "Okay. Wait. Kissing seems pretty definitive. Why don't you know?"

"We haven't talked about it since. He's acting like nothing ever happened."

"Maybe he doesn't know how to bring it up."

"Well, that makes two of us."

"So do you want to wear a different dress so that you'll look ugly and repel him, or do you want to look hot?"

I laughed nervously. I didn't know how to think about that. Did I want to look "hot" for Wesley? "Hot" and "Wesley" were not words that ever used to go together.

But I definitely didn't want to repel him.

"I want to look good."

"But not like you're trying to look good?"

I snapped my fingers. "Exactly."

Savannah rifled through my closet. She knew most of what I had—she'd certainly borrowed enough of it over the years—but she didn't seem to be looking for something in particular. She pulled out a few things, held them up in front of me, returned them, and repeated the process multiple times before pulling out my pastel green dress with a floral pattern on it and tossing the hanger over my neck.

"That with your brown ankle boots."

"Boots?"

She nodded. "The dress is really nice, so the boots will dress it down. But you'll still look killer."

I held the dress against my hips and looked down at it. "Are you sure?"

She nodded again. "So Wesley, huh? Can't say I'm surprised."

"Really? I am."

"That's because you're clueless."

I rolled my eyes. "Gee, thanks."

"He's obviously had a thing for you for, like, years."

"He has?"

She sat down on the chair by my closet. "You mean you never noticed?"

I shrugged. "I mean, I guess when we were younger, I thought maybe it was a possibility, but he never said anything or did anything, so I assumed I was wrong."

"When was he supposed to say something? In middle school? Or maybe later when you were dating Sean? Or maybe after that when you moped for weeks?"

"I did not mope over Sean."

"Or maybe later when you became set on moving hours away from him?"

I lowered my voice and said, "I wasn't trying to move away from him, you know."

"Does it matter though? You'd still be moving."

UF was the dream. It had always been the dream. I could picture myself in a dorm room, walking that campus, graduating, applying to law school, even living in Gainesville permanently. But in all of that picturing I'd done, I never pictured Wesley wouldn't be there.

Then again, I guess I never pictured him there either. He was always at UT. I'd never given any thought to what that would mean for our friendship.

"Have you told him yet?" Savannah asked, a hint of judgment in her voice.

I evaded her question. "Green dress it is."

***

"Turn left at the next light," Wesley said.

"Seriously? You're really going to direct this way the entire time?"

"I have to maintain the surprise."

"This isn't a big town, you know. There are only so many places to go. Eventually I'll figure it out."

"Straight through this light then right at the next."

"You're really not going to tell me?"

In response, Wesley just laughed.

We drove in silence for a few minutes at that point since Wesley didn't give directions for a little while. Other than directions, arguing about whether or not he was going to tell me where we were going, and talking about the concert that night, we hadn't really talked. It made me wonder if that meant this was just like Savannah had first said—that this was normal, something we did all the time, and not at all related to the kiss. That same cologne from the other day and his navy button-down shirt with the sleeves rolled up told me otherwise.

But maybe he was just dressing for the concert?

I couldn't ignore how much this felt like a date. If I was going to date Wesley for real, I needed to be honest, and I needed to do it before I lost my nerve.

"Wesley, we need to talk about something—"

"Left at the Dunkin and park."

I said, "Park at the Dunkin? That's your big surprise? Donuts?"

He scoffed. "You think so little of me? I meant park in that giant grass lot."

I looked where he was pointing and saw a huge lot that was already mostly filled. We weren't far from downtown, so it was possible that this was overflow parking from the shops and restaurants there since there was never enough parking downtown, but I couldn't be sure.

And I'd missed another chance.

I'd barely put the truck in park when Wesley flung his door open and bolted around the side to open mine. He'd done that before either in a joking way or because my father was watching, but he'd never done it seriously and voluntarily before.

"By the way," he said, "did I say earlier that you look nice tonight?"

I wasn't going to be the first to blink. "Thought I should dress up for the concert."

He smiled, but it didn't look the same. "Of course."

"You look good, too."

He shrugged. "Concert."

We walked over to the park that sits just outside downtown, and there seemed to be some kind of festival or event happening. There were musicians on street corners, food vendors selling all kinds of surely unhealthy but tasty finger foods, and what looked like a bonfire in the center of the park. Downtown was hardly a downtown because it was so small, but whenever they did events like this, it was always really cool.

"What is this?" I asked.

"Your surprise."

I rolled my eyes. "Yeah, I got that. But what is this festival for?"

He shrugged. "I think it's some music thing, but the food is the big draw here. They've got a lot of really good stuff."

Music festival? The same night as our concert? "Do you think this will hurt our attendance tonight? I mean, these are real musicians."

"And we're not? Relax, it won't hurt us at all."

I tried to let it go, but I was worried about our concert, and I couldn't help feeling like something had shifted between us. When I detracted from the compliment he gave me, I had expected him to argue or say something sassy or react in some way. Instead, he had kind of shut down. I didn't know why, and that didn't make figuring out what we were any easier. It also didn't make telling him about UF any easier.

Wesley immediately led me over to a food stall that was serving empanadas knowing my great affinity for them and ordered more than we could realistically eat. I mocked him for ordering such an absurd amount—who could possibly eat twelve empanadas?—but he insisted it was absolutely necessary.

"One of each flavor," he said.

"Neither one of us even likes mushrooms though."

He shrugged. "Gotta get the full experience."

After we had finished gorging ourselves on a medley of empanadas, we decided to take a walk to work off some of the overly full feeling we both had now. We circled the bonfire, and even though it was already a thousand degrees outside because it was March in Florida, the heat from the bonfire still felt good in that way that only fire does. I'd always liked the smell of wood burning, so I relished the strong scent.

"This is cool," I said. "I don't think I've ever been to this festival."

"I think it's new. I'm glad you like it."

I couldn't take it anymore. I had to take the risk. He was acting so strangely, and the not knowing was driving me insane. I hoped this wouldn't impact our friendship because the thought of losing Wesley or even damaging our friendship was more painful than I wanted to consider, but I had to hope that having this conversation would fix things in the long run. I glanced around to see if anyone was too close, and when I saw some freshmen girls from our school standing nearby, I took Wesley's hand and led him over to the other side of the bonfire. That same spark happened when I touched his hand, further warmed by the heat from the fire, and I finally knew I was hoping for something more than just our continued friendship.

"What is it?" Wesley said, looking down at our interlaced fingers.

"I need to ask you something."

Wesley looked nervous. "Okay."

"Are you into me?"

"Uh—"

"Because we kissed, and you totally didn't disagree with Barbara's comment, but then you never said anything or *did* anything, and I've been trying to figure out this whole time what's going on between us, and I don't know how to dress around you anymore, and Savannah thinks you've liked me for a long time, but now you're being weird, and I don't know why, but the Strawberry Festival was really great and—"

Wesley took my chin in both of his hands and kissed me so suddenly that I was still trying to talk at first before I became so utterly distracted by his lips on mine and his fingers on the sides of my neck. I became aware that my hands were still up in whatever frantic gesture I had been making while talking, so I rested them hesitantly on his waist, reaching around to his back. The heat from the flames crackling next to us was getting a little too strong, but I didn't have any desire to move, and it seemed like Wesley didn't either.

After a few moments—and oddly, I made note of the fact that it was a few moments longer than last time since I knew Taylor would ask—he pulled back without removing his hands, so I didn't either.

He said, "I didn't mean to—"

"I know."

"I hope it's okay."

"It is."

"I didn't know how else to—"

"Yeah," I said with a smile.

He let out a small huff. "I thought I had totally freaked you out at the Strawberry Festival."

"Why?"

"Well, you didn't really say anything the rest of the night."

"Neither did you."

"Or all weekend."

"Again, neither did you."

Wesley scratched the back of his neck. "I didn't know what to say. And then it was all about the project, so I thought maybe you were avoiding talking about it. So I thought asking you to prom would be an easy way to see how you felt, but you were so weird about it, so I wasn't sure."

"I was surprised," I said. "We hadn't talked about the kiss, and then we were suddenly going to prom. I didn't know if we were going as friends or dates."

He nodded. "I don't know, I guess it just seemed like you were trying to friend zone me or something. You never seemed to react to anything."

"Like what?"

He gestured around us. "Like me asking you on a date."

"I wasn't sure that it was one. We have dinner together all the time."

"Or when I complimented your dress earlier."

"I was trying to figure out if you were flirting."

"Well apparently I wasn't flirting very successfully since I was doing overtime, and you didn't get any of it."

At that, we both dissolved into laughter. The entire thing was so ridiculous, really. How had we so completely misunderstood each other?

"We're so bad at this," I said in between fits of giggles.

Wesley wiped a tear from his eye. "The worst."

Once we both settled down, I took his hand in mine. "So what now?"

"Empanadas round two?"

"You know that's not what I mean."

He shrugged. "We go to prom? Dare I say a second date?"

"Just like that? That simple?"

"Why not?"

I smiled and gladly accepted the hug he offered. Hugging wasn't new to us, but this feeling of comfort and affection and closeness was. When someone behind us tossed some extra branches onto the bonfire, I turned to watch, keeping my head on his shoulder. I'd never put my head on Wesley's shoulder before except for maybe falling asleep on him on a school bus or something, so I'd never noticed how perfectly we seemed to fit together until the Strawberry Festival when we were on the Ferris wheel. It felt just as natural and right now. He wrapped his arm around my waist, so I slipped my hand into the hand on my hip.

Wesley said, "So, uh, how long has Savannah known?"

I felt suddenly flushed. Was he talking about UF? How did he find out? Was he mad? Disappointed? And which of those was worse? The tone of his voice was pretty unreadable, and I didn't know what to expect. I tried not to grip his arms noticeably. "About what?"

He chuckled. "About the kiss." Then, after clearing his throat, he added. "That I liked you."

I smiled even though he couldn't see it and felt my pulse slow down. He hadn't found out. At least not yet. Was it only a matter of time? It was feeling more and more impossible to keep the secret in. The anxiety was eating me alive. But the way his arm felt wrapped around my waist made it that much harder to admit to my mounting deception. "Not sure. She just said that she thought you liked me for years."

"Years? Shoot, I'm not nearly as subtle as I thought I was."

"So she's right? Years?"

He hesitated. "I didn't say that."

I pulled back and made eye contact. "You're caught now, Dixon."

He sighed. "I was afraid to say something. Didn't want to hurt our friendship."

"Same."

"Besides, I thought we'd graduate and be hours apart."

I nodded. "That's what Savannah thought. But we had all of high school. You could've said something."

"I guess. I just didn't want to stand in the way of UF. It's so important to you."

"But now you don't mind standing in the way?"

"I didn't mean it like that. I just—I guess I got caught up in the moment."

There was that gnawing feeling in my gut that had popped up in recent days. I still hadn't found a way to tell Wesley about UF. If everything went according to plan, I could still get in, and he would never know. And then what would happen? Would I leave, go to UF, prove to Wesley that he was right to avoid pursuing me since it could only end in my leaving? Or would we struggle to maintain a long distance relationship? Maybe this relationship never even would have happened if he had known, and maybe I was dooming it before it could start if I told him now. Was I selfish for wanting to keep him in the dark so that I could keep him in my arms? It was starting to feel like no matter what I did, Wesley was going to end up hurt, and I didn't know how to prevent it or even how to voice it to him. Normally, he would've been the person I'd go to to ask for advice or help, but I didn't know who to go to when the advice I most needed was about him.

Finally, I said, "I'm glad you did," and it was true. I was glad he'd gotten caught up in the moment and kissed me on a whim. I didn't regret it, and as long as I could help it, I would enjoy every kiss, embrace, and smile with him that I could.

14

— · —

Wesley and I left the park early to make sure we wouldn't get caught in traffic on the way to Evan's. We wanted to be there early, and since we seemed to be in the habit now of getting distracted by each other, we needed to make sure we could stay on task.

Evan and Alfredo already had all the lights turned on, so even from the street, you could see the glow in the back lot. Evan's friends were testing the sound equipment, and while Alfredo and Rhett poured extra cups of water, a few of the other cast members started to arrive. It occurred to me that Wesley and I hadn't discussed the social situation. Were we going to tell people that we were together? We'd been holding hands when we first got here, but now we were busy getting some stuff set up. Would we hold hands later in front of all of our classmates? Would he kiss me? Would people react? Did I care if they did?

"Wow, Jorie," Rachel said, "you and Wesley did a great job with this. It's beautiful out here."

"Thanks, but honestly Evan and Rhett did most of the setup."

"Still, the idea is so cool. I'm really excited about it."

"Me, too."

Rachel's eyes widened. "Oh, and I hear from Drew that you and Wesley are going with us in the limo for prom. That's so exciting!"

"Yeah, I can't believe you didn't tell me you were going with Drew. How did that happen?"

Rachel blushed and smiled. "He asked me the other day after school. It was so sweet. He bought flowers and everything."

"Wow."

"Yeah. But I'm really excited that you're joining us. That will be so much more fun." She looked around and lowered her voice. "Are you two a thing?"

I didn't know what to say. We hadn't decided what we would say. Finally, I decided that Rachel wasn't exactly a gossip anyway. "Yeah, I guess we are."

Rachel gasped as her eyes widened even further, if that was humanly possible. "That's fantastic! Y'all are so cute together."

"Jorie," Sienna said as she sauntered in between me and Rachel, and I nearly choked on her Bath and Body Works perfume. "So good to see you. I wasn't sure if you'd be here."

I said, "I literally planned this event. Why wouldn't I be here?"

She flipped her hair practically into Rachel's face. "Well, I wasn't sure if you were feeling up to it. You know, with how busy you've been."

I was about to tell her off when Wesley came over with a big smile. "Hey Rachel. Sienna, I'm so glad I ran into you. Caroline and I finished painting the Mrs. Potts costume, and Mr. King happily brought it tonight."

Sienna's mouth hung open. "He what?"

Wesley nodded cheerfully. "Yeah. See, after he heard how Rachel wore a yellow dress to Moe's the other night and just looked absolutely perfect as Belle, we thought it would be cool if a bunch of us dressed in costume, so I've got some boots to put on, Drew has this really cool jacket and fake sideburns, and Jamar is going to hold fake flames.

Lucky you, though, since you're the only one who has her costume already done. Let Caroline and me know if you want us to make any adjustments. Mr. King is waiting for you around back."

"You've got to be kidding me."

"You should know Mr. King never jokes."

Sienna didn't walk away right away, but finally she stormed off, and Rachel and I managed to contain our laughter only until she was just out of range. If Mr. King really made her wear that teapot, she would be seething on stage, and it would be glorious.

Once I had finally stopped laughing, I said, "How did you talk Mr. King into that?"

"Oh, I wasn't lying. I actually did tell him about Rachel's dress the other night, and he got totally into the idea. It just so happens to be that Sienna's costume is the worst, so Caroline and I made sure we finished it first."

"Wesley, we owe you a debt of gratitude," Rachel said.

He bowed dramatically, and put on his Gaston voice to say, "Anything for you, dear Belle."

She curtsied back, and then headed over to the stage presumably to talk to Mr. King. Wesley hopped up to sit on the half wall along the edge of the property and smiled. He looked so good when he smiled. I wanted to kiss him right there in front of everybody, but I refrained.

"You okay?" he asked.

I nodded. "Just Sienna being Sienna."

"Doesn't mean it isn't annoying."

I bit the inside of my cheek. "It's not that big of a deal."

Wesley smiled again, then said, "Well, then I've got news for you."

"What's that?"

"Gian Frances is here."

"Really?"

Gian Frances was Wesley's theater director at the River Glen Community Theater. Wesley had been participating in their summer productions ever since he was a little kid. Gian Frances had been directing there for years, almost the entire time Wesley had been performing there. He usually came to the River Glen Academy performances to see Wesley and a few of our other classmates who also did community theater, but it was interesting that he came to this concert.

Wesley said, "I asked him to come to support the event, and he even brought a few of the other directors and musicians from the theater. I was just hoping they'd come, maybe donate some money, let me hang a few flyers at the theater, but Gian just told me that he wants to donate some costumes."

"What?"

He nodded. "The theater did *Beauty and the Beast* a long time ago when I was a kid. I think I was a random teacup or something."

"How adorable."

He rolled his eyes. "He says they don't have all the costumes anymore since they repurposed some for other productions, and he says a few of them might be kind of dated for what we want, but he says you and I and maybe Mr. King should meet him there tomorrow to see what they have. It's a direct donation to Spotlight Heroes."

"That's incredible."

"It gets better. He says they're ours to keep. He says most of them haven't been used in years, so he doesn't mind letting them go and cleaning up the storage closets a little bit. So if we need to make any alterations, we can."

I hugged Wesley, and he lifted me off the ground for just a moment. "That's perfect. So if any are kind of weird, we can adjust them."

"Yeah, and Mr. King can hang on to them for the future. I mean, other than the furniture, a lot of those costumes would be pretty normal. They could be reused for other musicals."

"Definitely. That's a huge score. Did you tell Mr. King?"

He shook his head. "I literally just found out and was coming over to tell you when I saw Sienna harassing you."

"I guess you and Caroline didn't need to finish her costume then."

"Actually, it's good that we did. Gian says a lot of the furniture costumes got deconstructed to use for other things. We still need to build those."

"But that's totally doable. I mean, we already have Mrs. Potts and Chip and Lumiere."

He nodded. "And I convinced Devon and Caroline to work on the wardrobe and feather duster. It'll come together. But now we can actually have cool costumes. We can get a cool Beast costume for Drew and some wigs and dresses for the bimbettes."

"And a real ball gown for Rachel. It's going to be perfect."

"Plus this saves us some money that we need to fundraise. We'll be able to reach our goal now."

I threw my arms around Wesley's neck, and he lifted me off the ground in an embrace that, if anyone had been looking, would have definitely spelled "couple."

"We might actually win this thing," Wesley said.

"Oh, we'll definitely win now. We have to."

"Excuse me."

I turned around to see Mrs. Gonzalez waving with a big smile on her face.

"Mrs. Gonzalez," I said. "You remember Wesley Dixon?"

"Of course. Hello again."

"Hello," he said.

"This is a wonderful idea, and so creative. I'm glad to see you partnering with the local businesses. This has been a rough time economically for so many, so it's nice that you've both found a way to support your own musical while also supporting local businesses."

"Thank you."

"I gave it a lot of thought, and I'm happy to present you with a check. I am really hoping that the musical will come through, but if it doesn't, please don't return the money. Put it toward something else in the theater department. Next year's production, maybe? But after seeing this event, I'm confident it will move forward."

She handed me an envelope, and I shook her hand. "Thank you so much. I really appreciate that."

"Of course. I'm happy to help. And I see a lot of alumni here tonight. Was that planned?"

I nodded. "I invited them hoping to remind them of their on-stage glories."

Mrs. Gonzalez laughed. "You're a very driven young lady. I hope this works out for you. Now, if you'll excuse me, I'm going to take a seat before this starts. Good luck!"

As soon as she walked away, I tore open the envelope with Wesley hovering over my shoulder. I took one look at the check and nearly screamed.

"$1500!"

"Yes!" Wesley said.

"This is incredible."

"We can probably get other sponsors on board after a donation like that."

"Hey, what if the donors got rewards for donating? Big charities do stuff like that. They have brackets, and each bracket comes with prizes."

"But what could we offer?"

I shrugged. "Free attendance at the musical? Preferential seating?"

"Free concessions?"

I snapped my fingers. "Yes, that's good. Their business advertised in the playbill."

"And on the screen before the musical starts."

"Yes, that's really good."

Wesley smirked. "This is going to work."

I smiled and nodded. "It just might."

***

The concert went perfectly. Evan's friends were all spectacular, and they served as a good buffer in between all of the high schoolers performing. Rachel awed everyone, as expected, and her duet with Drew was swoon-worthy. Wesley and Jamar drew at least twice the laughs as they did at Moe's. Sienna's performance was highly entertaining and amusing, though I felt quite certain that that wasn't what she wanted. She spent most of the performance bumping into mic stands and fidgeting with her costume. Wesley managed to drag me on stage to fawn over him during his performance "to give the full Gaston effect" as he put it. Even the students playing minor characters performed well enough to garner some attention. I watched during all of the performances as people continued to drop money into the little buckets on the table. Plus, Alfredo was selling a ton of drinks and food, so I knew there was commission coming in from that. At Moe's, even though people were donating, it ended up being a lot less than it looked like at first because there were so many ones, but even if that was the case here, it still seemed like a lot. I tried not to get my hopes up, but it looked really promising.

Plus, with donated costumes, we just dropped a significant amount of money that had to be raised. I'd have to do the exact calculations later of how much we saved, but it was substantial. It got me thinking: what if theaters shared resources like this more often? Why should every school in the area buy costumes for *The Sound of Music* when the same costumes could be rotated around based on who's doing the production when? River Glen Community Theater was a pretty cool place, but it wasn't like they were rolling in cash either. This was extremely generous of them, especially given how much they've struggled in the past financially. I'm sure Mr. King would be willing to pay this forward down the line. Spotlight Heroes could coordinate stuff like that in the future. If a nonprofit oversees the transfers like that, I had to believe that more schools and companies would be willing to share. Mr. King had originally planned to get costumes from a consignment shop. I bet they would still be willing to donate and help out not just our school but others as well as local theaters. This idea was bigger than Wesley and I had planned, bigger than River Glen Academy or *Beauty and the Beast*. With the right organization, this business had the potential to become so much bigger. And the bigger it got, the more impressive it became for Dale Henchard of River Glen AutoMall, and more importantly, for the University of Florida. If I'd had any doubts previously about my ability to win this competition and get back on track at UF, this certainly dispelled them.

15

Wesley and I met up with Gian at the local theater the next day after breakfast to go over costumes. Mr. King had wanted to come, but he had to go to his daughter's soccer game, so he gave Wesley and me free rein to make decisions on costumes. Wesley had expressed some apprehension about making all of the decisions, but personally, I was thrilled. This gave Spotlight Heroes the final authority on costumes, which is exactly what I wanted. The more control that Spotlight Heroes could have, the better it would look for the competition.

Gian led us to one of the storage rooms in the basement of the theater. Even though it was just a community theater, the actual building was pretty nice. I guess it used to be a pretty official theater before the big one opened downtown, so even though the building was just hosting small community productions, the resources were pretty great.

Gian pushed a door open revealing more costumes than I thought possible to be crammed in a room this size. It seemed about the size of one of our classrooms but utterly packed with materials. It would take Wesley and I hours just to sort through everything.

Gian said, "I think most if not all of the *Beauty and the Beast* stuff is in here. If there's anything you don't see that you were hoping for, let me know, and I'll check the other rooms. Like I said, we deconstructed a few, so we don't have everything, but I'm happy to see what we have. Feel free to borrow some of the props, too, if you want. I'll be in my office."

With that, Gian left Wesley and I with the overwhelming task of wading into this costume chaos. We decided that the most efficient strategy would be to start on opposite sides of the room and work toward each other to meet in the center back of the room. The idea was reasonable in theory, but in practice, we found it harder to execute than we had realized. Because the room wasn't organized, it was difficult to identify what exactly was Wesley's side and what was mine. We ended up bumping into each other more than once, which, honestly, I didn't exactly mind.

After probably fifteen minutes or so, Wesley let out a huff. "I know there's good stuff in here, but it's impossible to find anything in here. I feel like it'd be easier and faster just to clean the entire room."

"Are you volunteering?"

"You know what I mean."

I nodded. "Okay, new game plan. We start by looking for obvious stuff: Belle's gold dress, obnoxiously loud dresses for the bimbettes, anything that looks like furniture. Those things will be easier to spot, I think, than normal stuff like white dress shirts and a regular blue dress."

"Seems logical."

"Okay, I'll climb over these boxes and look in the back. You stay in the front."

"You sure you want to brave the unknown back there?"

I laughed. "I think I'll survive."

This strategy wasn't significantly better, but it was better, I supposed, since it seemed like we were covering more ground. We found a few white dress shirts that would be perfect for Belle's father Maurice, Gaston, the Beast, and LeFou, and enough shirts in different colors for the townspeople and the furniture in the castle after they come back to life. We found some wigs that would probably work for something, and a blue dress that would definitely not fit Rachel but could probably be altered to fit well enough. Ugly ball gowns weren't hard to find, and we had more than we needed. The elusive piece was the ball gown for Belle. We'd found several beautiful ball gowns, but they were all either the wrong shape or style or they weren't gold.

I sat down on a box and sighed. "What do we do?"

He shrugged. "Maybe we'll just have to buy that dress by itself."

"A really pretty ball gown could easily cost $500. I don't want to have to fundraise that money if we don't have to."

Wesley picked up one of the discarded dresses. "It's too bad most of these are white. Some of them would look great."

It was true. Many of them had the perfect volume or ruching. I could picture some of them on Rachel. They had probably been used as wedding dresses in previous productions. At least one of them was probably from *Cinderella*. It seemed that Gian had everything except the exact dress we wanted.

"I know," I said before hopping up off the box. "Come on, let's go check the prop room. We'll come back to the dress."

The prop room was next door and significantly larger though much better organized. This room housed mostly small props, so luckily we didn't have to wade through furniture, though all the shelving units made the room feel just about as cramped. Most of the shelves were labeled, and nearly everything was displayed, so there were very few boxes that needed rifling. We found everything we needed: books, gadgets, swords, small furniture and decor items, fake food, even things we didn't think we needed until we saw them.

Wesley was sorting through the fake flowers looking for an enchanted rose when I spotted a box labeled "Beauty/Beast." That seemed promising enough. I popped the box open and found some duplicates of the stuff we already had, but I also found a big, gorgeous fake rose in a plastic case that definitely looked and felt like glass. I called Wesley's name so he would take the rose, but just as he walked over, I spotted some glittering fabric at the bottom underneath some cotton sheets. I shoved the cotton at Wesley and reached for the gold fabric.

Wesley started, "Is that—"

Before he could finish, I unfurled a beautiful gold ball gown. It was even prettier than any of the white dresses we had seen. It was big and dramatic but not stiff or overwhelming, and the rouching all the way down made it look fancier than it was. It was off-the-shoulder, and the top layer of fabric was this gauzy gold mesh that was covered in glitter. Even in this dark prop room, it was glistening at every bit of light. I couldn't even begin to imagine how spectacular it would look under spotlights.

"It's perfect."

Wesley nodded. "Will it fit her?"

I stood and held it up against my body. Rachel was taller than me by several inches, but judging by the way it was dragging on the ground when against me, that wouldn't be a problem. Other than height, we were probably about the same size, and it seemed like it would fit me. If it didn't fit Rachel, it would be close enough to alter. The more I examined it, the more I spotted some minor damaged pieces of fabric, snags, or stains, but I was confident that they weren't detrimental to the dress. This was the perfect Belle dress.

Wesley said, "I wonder why this wasn't in the costume room."

"I think because it's so obviously a Belle dress. Someone just decided to keep it with the other *Beauty and the Beast* stuff."

"Well that's huge. Is there anything else we even need?"

I grabbed a spare hanger to hang the dress. It had some lines on it from being folded that we'd probably have to steam out. "I don't think so. I mean, we still need a few things, but it's all little stuff."

"Looks like we were right. We'll still have to build all the furniture costumes."

"Yeah, but that's not a big deal."

"Awesome."

"Should we start loading the truck?"

He nodded, but instead of moving toward the door, he suddenly dumped everything he was holding onto the shelf next to him and looped his arm around my waist and kissed me. A quick one, just because, and I couldn't help smiling.

Wesley picked up the stuff he had dumped and smirked. "Now I'm ready to load the truck."

Wesley piled his arms up with all of the stuff he'd been holding and looked back long enough to give me a wink. Sometimes I really had to wonder how I had never realized this before. I hadn't really known that he liked me, hadn't given myself permission to ask myself if I could like him, and I couldn't help but wonder how much time we had missed out on. It seemed inconceivable now that we hadn't always been this way: giving each other winks, sending flirty text messages, kissing whenever we felt like it. It was perfect this way. As I watched him walk out the door with an armful of frilly dresses, I wondered how I'd gotten so lucky. I could only hope that I wasn't destroying everything we'd become.

***

Back at my house, Wesley and I started sorting through everything we'd pulled from the theater. We hadn't put much thought into transporting everything other than keeping it safe and getting it here, but now we had a jumbled mess. We had tried to enlist Savannah's help, but as little sisters often do, she claimed that we were taking advantage of her and locked herself in her room. We had completely covered my living room in costumes and props, and I was pretty sure that Mom wouldn't be happy about how much glitter was getting on the couch, but there was really no better way to do this.

We piled all of the small props onto the coffee table, laying the dresses out according to major, minor, and choral roles on the couch, and Wesley organized the men's costumes on the lounge chair. It was chaos, but it was slowly becoming organized chaos.

I hadn't really floated my idea about expanding the business and therefore the project to Wesley yet. I'd had to do some pretty serious arm-twisting to get him to agree to this, so I wasn't sure how he'd react to the suggestion of diving in deeper. I also didn't know how flirting and kissing affected our decision making abilities. Or hidden lies.

"So I was thinking about the project at the concert the other night."

Wesley was focused on his task, so he didn't even look over. "Yeah?"

"Remember when Mr. King wanted to do *The Wizard of Oz*?"

He laughed. "Yeah, that was a trainwreck if I ever saw one."

"Well sure, Sienna had no business being Glinda."

"She was a witch though."

I suppressed the urge to snort. "True. But we've never used those costumes again."

"Yeah, well how else do you repurpose witch dresses and munchkin costumes?"

"I bet Gian could use that kind of stuff."

"Maybe."

I'm just thinking that such a big part of our problem was fixed just by a donation of stuff from another struggling theater. Couldn't we return the favor?"

"Yeah, sure, ask Mr. King about it."

"That's not what I mean. I mean, what if we incorporated that into Spotlight Heroes?"

This time he did stop what he was doing. "What do you mean?"

"I mean, why should we only benefit River Glen Academy's theater program? This was about saving the arts, right? Protecting this thing that meant a lot to a lot of people. The community theater is important, too. What if we tried to fundraise and support stuff like that? We could expand to include community theaters, other small private schools, maybe even youth arts programs—"

"Whoa, whoa." Wesley held up his hands. "Don't you think you're getting a little ahead of yourself?"

"Obviously our number one goal is still the school musical, but think how much better our project would look if we did more than that? Even if we don't finish everything in time for the competition, if we can show that we started the expansion, it would look really cool."

"Yeah, it would, but that's a whole other project."

"But think about all of the other community theaters and schools in this area that just don't have the funding. Don't you want to help them, too?"

"You know I do, but we just don't have the time for that. Besides, we're not even an official organization yet. The IRS hasn't technically approved us yet."

"Yeah, but as you said, it's a technicality, a formality. It'll come through. But we could pretty much guarantee a win this way."

Wesley shifted back and forth. "You know I never really wanted to win. I just wanted the extra credit."

"Well, I want to win."

"Why?"

I could see him pulling back, pulling away from me. It wasn't physical, but I could sense the distance between us, and I knew I was the reason for it. I was pushing Wesley away.

"Just because."

"But why?"

I bit my lip. I wanted to tell him, but it seemed like a pointless thing to bring up now. What if it endangered our entire relationship? What if it made this crevice forming between us turn into a trench, one we couldn't cross? "I just really think it'll look great for both of us. Plus, it helps the arts. Win-win."

"I don't know, Jorie."

"Come on, just think how great it would be."

"I just really don't know if all that's feasible right now. We've still got rehearsals for the musical, school, work, prom, us. I don't know if I can handle more right now."

I took his hand in mine. "Will you at least think about it?"

Wesley agreed to think about it, and we went back to sorting, but I wasn't confident in the outcome. It didn't seem like Wesley was on board at all, and I couldn't drag him along this time. If he didn't agree to move forward, what would happen? What would I do?

I decided that if Wesley wouldn't help me, I would make it happen myself. One way or another, I was going to win that competition. I was frustrated that he was not only doubting our current project but casting doubt on any future idea I came up with, but I didn't really need him anymore. If Wesley was part of the puzzle of getting there—and I certainly hoped he would be—then all the better, but if I had to do it without his help, then so be it.

16

I was up all night that night unable to sleep and unable to stop thinking about Wesley, UF, the project, Spotlight Heroes, the musical, everything. In all of the chaos, I'd forgotten my ultimate goal here: to get into UF. The project was a means to an end. I hadn't expected to get so caught up in the project or to like running Spotlight Heroes as much as I did, but it was no use denying now that I did enjoy it. I liked knowing I was making a difference. I liked seeing the cast getting so excited about the musical in a way that I had never seen before. I wanted to spread this work around to other schools and organizations so that they could benefit, too.

But ultimately, the mission was UF. Not only had I found something I enjoyed, but more importantly, I had found a way to take something I enjoyed and use it to my advantage. This would be my ticket to UF, and I knew it.

Resigned to the fact that I wouldn't be able to sleep, I sat up and grabbed my laptop from my nightstand and started poring over my spreadsheets, budgets, and write-ups for Spotlight Heroes. As part of my negotiations with Wesley, I had agreed to do most of the academic work associated with the project, especially for the parts I had expanded. He was in charge of the more visual elements of the presentation since he was more artistically gifted than I was, and I agreed to do all the writing. I had already finished most of it. Once we met our fundraising goal and organized everything, I would have to finish the write-up, but this was everything we had so far.

The concert had brought in a substantial amount, and combined with our profits from Moe's, we were nearly halfway through our revised goal ever since we got free costumes. More importantly, this had been enough not only to convince Mr. Quentin to allow the musical to continue, but it had convinced some of the donors Mr. King had previously lost to rejoin the donations efforts. I was optimistic that we'd have everything we needed within two weeks, and since the musical was still more than three weeks away, we would have everything we needed. If we were still short, I was confident that we'd be able to convince a few more donors to chip in the rest.

I spent longer than I should have fiddling with the spreadsheets before finally shutting my laptop. I flopped back down on my pillow, but my stomach still felt uneasy. I didn't know what to do about Wesley. I'd gotten swept up in my newfound feelings for Wesley without ever considering the consequences. What did it really mean to date your best friend? Were we ruining our friendship? What about when Wesley found out the truth? And what would happen when I moved to Gainesville to attend UF? It wasn't just four years: my plans included law school at UF as well. I was looking at potentially seven years in a city far away from the one Wesley planned to live in for at least four years. And who knew where we would end up after that? I had no intentions of leaving Florida, but Wesley had never really made up his mind. We never made each other any kind of promise to stay close in college—I think we both just kind of assumed that we would. Now everything was so much more complex, and it definitely didn't feel like that had made anything any simpler. Agreeing to stay friends was one thing, but agreeing to date long-distance? That was a completely different matter. It seemed like there was absolutely nothing to indicate that this relationship had any chance of lasting.

A small but loud part of my brain, or maybe my heart, kept tugging and saying, *But what about right now?* Was it really fair to throw away the chance at an entire relationship just because it might not work seven years from now? Was I being too much of a planner, as usual? It wasn't in my nature to be spontaneous or rash or even to enjoy something short-term if I thought it wouldn't work long-term. This was only magnified when talking about romantic relationships. Wasn't there just something to love that was, by nature, spontaneous, rash, and enjoyable?

And did I just use the word "love" when trying to decipher my feelings for Wesley?

Frustrated, I made my way to the kitchen and scoured for something to eat. My mom was a habitual baker, so there had to be something. I wasn't having much luck, and the only thing I could find was my dad's secret can of fudge frosting, and I knew better than to touch that. Maybe this was a sign to be healthier and avoid eating a ton of processed sugar at 1am. I was about to resign myself to my dessertless fate when my mom walked in.

"Hi, sweetie, is everything okay?"

"Yeah," I said with an attempt at a casual tone. "Just couldn't sleep."

Mom opened the fridge, pulled out a foil-covered bowl, grabbed two big spoons, and leaned across the counter. I accepted the spoon but waited with confusion to see what was in the bowl. When she uncovered it and revealed a giant batch of chocolate chip cookie dough, I nearly cheered. She must have seen the expression on my face, and she shrugged. "Haven't had a chance to bake them yet. So, is something on your mind?"

I shoved my spoon in and scooped a giant scoop. "Nothing major. Just a lot of little things."

"Are they little if they're keeping you up at night?"

I rolled my eyes. "It's not that big of a deal, Mom, I promise. It's fine."

"If you say so."

We ate cookie dough in silence for a few moments. I was afraid she would bring up UF. I never told them—I'd mostly just been avoiding talking to them about college at all—and I certainly didn't want to talk about it now. I had wondered if Savannah told them, but Savannah likely knew better than to spill a secret like that to our parents. Just more people being added to the list I was hiding from.

I'd been avoiding one-on-one conversations with Mom to avoid having to talk about it. It felt like she was going to bring it up, but eventually, Mom just said, "You know what might help you sleep?"

"What?"

"Packing for the USF trip."

"It's just an overnight trip. Doesn't require that much effort to pack."

"Well, then maybe it'll get your mind off of whatever you can't stop thinking about."

I scooped up a final scoop. "I guess it can't hurt."

Mom returned the cookie dough to the fridge, swore me to secrecy, and headed back to bed. Reluctantly, I took her advice and decided to pack. It was obvious that I wasn't going to be able to sleep, so at least this way I could be productive.

I still didn't want to go on this trip, but there was no talking Mom out of it. She was determined to show me the USF campus. Fine. If seeing the campus would get her to back off finally, then okay. We'd go, we'd look at the campus, I'd comment on how nice the library looks, Dad would make some weird jokes about the contemporary art museum, Savannah would beg to see the medical buildings, and then we'd leave. We'd probably drive by UT as well, even though I hadn't even applied there since it was so close. I'd picture Wesley walking that campus and wonder if he'd be thinking of me. Maybe it would be for the best if he wasn't thinking of me. Maybe this is where we should decide not to push this any further. Maybe the best option is for Wesley to be at UT, me to be at UF, and for us to see each other at Christmas and summer breaks.

I'd go on this trip to make everyone happy, but that's all it would be.

***

Wesley and I had plans to touch base after the concert and costume haul to figure out exactly where we stood. The musical was a couple of weeks away, and we had to have a progress report ready for Mr. King and Mr. Quentin the Monday after spring break. Since my family was going to Tampa for a few days at the beginning of spring break, and Wesley was going to be working for most of the week, we decided it would be a good idea to get together now and figure out what each of us needed to do so we could complete it independently. And since Wesley's car was still acting up, I drove to his house to make it easier.

Wesley's house was about as stereotypically country as it got. It was a farmhouse design that somehow looked bigger than it was. I always liked his house. It was such a pretty style. His mom had fantastic taste. I had probably just about as many good memories associated with this house as I did with my own house. Wesley and I practically grew up at each other's houses

I parked behind Wesley's car and waved to his dad who was working on his own car in the garage. For as long as I'd known Wesley, his dad had been working on that car. He'd been telling people for years that one day it would be a "real beaut." In eighth grade, Wesley and I had placed bets on when he would actually finish. With him guessing our junior year and me guessing our senior year, it looked like we were both going to lose.

"Marjorie," Mrs. Dixon said as she opened the front door with a big smile. "So nice to see you."

"You, too, Mrs. Dixon." Wesley's parents and my own were probably the only people I didn't mind using my full first name.

"I think Wesley is in the den. You can head on over there and track him down."

"Thank you."

"Let me know if y'all want any snacks."

I smiled. "We will."

The den of the house had doors to it, but they were French doors, so you could see through them. Sure enough, Wesley was sitting on the couch working on homework. His parents had bought him a desk that sat idle in his bedroom. He always said he couldn't properly work at a desk. I never really understood that, but to each his own, I guess.

As soon as I opened the door, he turned around, and when he saw me, his face broke into a smile. If he kept smiling like that, keeping my distance would be hard.

"You're early," he said.

"Avoiding USF trip planning."

"Ah, yes, the dreaded voyage. It probably won't be as bad as you think."

"USF, no. But my mother's attempts to sell me on USF? That will absolutely be as bad as I think."

He laughed, and when I sat down on the couch next to him, he leaned over and kissed me on the cheek. I wanted desperately to turn and kiss him for real, but I maintained my focus.

I said, "So, I brought you the revised spreadsheets based on our new costs since we got the costumes for free."

"Cool. Oh wait, I completely forgot to tell you."

"What?"

Wesley grabbed an envelope from the coffee table and handed it to me. It had a UT letterhead on it. At my raised eyebrows, he urged me to open it, so I did. I scanned the letter quickly, but I saw the word that mattered: scholarship.

"You won a scholarship?"

He nodded. "Merit-based."

"That's fantastic."

Another nod. "I guess being third in the class is still impressive, even if you don't beat out Ann for salutatorian."

"Well, I tried to tell you that."

"Anyway, it's a lot of money."

"Full tuition?"

He laughed. "Not that much money, but it's pretty substantial. It makes attending a private university not feel like a private university. My parents are through the roof."

"I bet." Wesley's parents were well off, but a private university was asking a lot. They knew how badly he wanted to go to UT, but I knew cost was a concern. Wesley had been applying to scholarships all year, but he had only won one for $500.

"It gets better. My parents were so happy that they decided to gift me the rest of the money I need to fix my car. They're matching what I had saved up, so I'm taking it over to the shop either today or tomorrow."

"Wow, great timing, during spring break and all."

"Yeah. You won't have to chauffeur me anymore."

"It's not like I minded."

He shrugged. "Still. Anyway, I didn't want to forget to tell you."

"That's great news. I'm really happy for you."

"Thanks."

"So, I think we should figure out what else we need to plan. We've got one more spirit night fundraiser set up, and I've been talking to some of the donors that Mr. King lost. I think those things combined should be enough to meet our revised goal. It looks like we don't have to worry about the musical anymore. The money is going to come through. We'll just have to write up the report."

"That's great."

"And we never really finished our conversation from the other day. About expanding to help out other organizations and schools."

Wesley shifted uncomfortably. "I still don't know about that. It's so much extra work. Besides, we got what we wanted. The musical is saved."

"That's not all we wanted. We still have the competition to think of. Yeah, fundraising to save the musical is cool, but is it impressive enough to win?"

"That's why we created Spotlight Heroes. The business is what's impressive."

"Yeah, but it could be so much more. We still have a few weeks. We could organize a few more events and maybe benefit the community theaters. We're already doing it. What's a few more events?"

Wesley's eyes widened. "A lot of work. These events have been great, but they've taken up all of our free time. I just don't think either of us has the time anymore."

"It's not that bad. It's not like we're working full-time jobs."

"We kind of are."

"But it would look so good. How could we lose?"

"I'm not so sure that winning is that important to me."

I sat back a little. "What?"

"I mean, I guess I was never as into the competition as you were."

"You're the one who wanted to do it in the first place! You talked me into it."

"Yeah, 'cause I thought it'd be fun, and I wanted the extra credit. But I don't really need it anymore."

"Oh, so you got a scholarship so you're just out?"

Wesley huffed. "I'm not skipping out on the project. Of course I'll help you finish and present the project for the competition, but I just don't think we need to be adding anything to it."

"So you're just giving up, then?"

"No, I just said—"

"You know, you wanted me to do this project, and ever since I agreed, you've been trying to undercut it."

His face twisted. "Undercut it?" And there it was. I hadn't ever admitted to myself really that I felt that way, but seeing the way he was looking at me—a disdainful look he had never directed at me before—made it painfully obvious. Despite the fact that I knew I was making things worse, I couldn't stop talking, couldn't stop heaping problem on top of problem.

"Yeah. You've never been as invested in this as I am. Every time I want to do something, you shoot it down."

"That is not true."

"I've been doing most of the work here."

"Excuse me? Who got the costumes for free? Who went with you to pick them out? Who finished building the other costumes? Who planned the concert? Who sang at all of the performances? I've been putting in a ton of work for this project. You just don't want to finish any one project. You just keep suggesting new things."

"And you don't even consider the ideas. You just automatically reject them because you claim you don't have time."

"I don't have time. And frankly, neither do you."

"You don't get to tell me what I do and don't have time for."

Wesley sighed, pinching the bridge of his nose. "Look, I wasn't trying to get into a fight with you. I was just saying that I don't think I can invest that kind of energy into more than we already agreed to. Sure, I wanted the extra credit and the prize, but we're still getting the extra credit, we could still win, and if we don't, that's okay. We saved the musical. That was the biggest reason we did this. We don't need to make this bigger than it is."

"Well, I need it." I could feel my face getting hot.

"Why?"

"I just do."

"Tell me why."

"To get into UF."

I had practically screamed the words, and once they were out and couldn't be taken back, I regretted them. Wesley looked shocked, but he maintained an unreadable expression. There it was in all its ugliness: the real reason I had agreed to do the project.

"What?"

I let out a small huff. "I didn't get accepted into UF. I got waitlisted." I felt my eyes stinging, but I refused to let myself cry. "They said that if anything changed on my application, then I could let them know and maybe get off the waitlist, so I was hoping this project would be that."

Wesley's voice was low. "Why didn't you tell me?"

"I mean, I knew you wanted the money for the car, and—"

"That's not what I'm asking."

My stomach twisted. Why *hadn't* I told him? I had promised myself that I would tell him when the time was right, but the timing never felt right. Besides, how do you tell your best friend that you're a failure? And how do you admit it after lying for a while? Maybe a few months ago I would've been able to tell him, but now? After everything that had happened between us? We weren't just friends anymore. We were something more, something I couldn't yet identify. I couldn't bear to look him in the eye and admit the ugly truth, but seeing the pain in his eyes right now made me wonder why I had ever thought lying to him was a good idea. "I didn't want you to know."

"Why? We tell each other everything. You just suddenly decided that you didn't trust me anymore? I thought I meant more to you than that."

He did. He did mean more than that. And that was the problem. "You know that you do."

Wesley let out a low laugh. "Do I?"

"I was embarrassed. I didn't want anyone to know."

"But I'm not 'anyone,' Jorie. You really thought I would—what—make fun of you? Shame you for not getting in? That's what Sienna would do, not me. Is that really what you think of me?"

"No, I just—"

"I can't believe you've been lying to me this whole time."

I could feel the heat in my face rising again. "UF is important to me. You should know that by now."

"I do know that."

"Then how could you possibly be mad that I did whatever it took to get in?"

"Jorie, I'm mad that you didn't tell me. If you had told me the truth, I would have done the project to help you." He rubbed his head and huffed. "Everything we've been doing for weeks has been a lie."

That hurt more than anything else he had said or I had done. Being angry at me was one thing. Thinking I had betrayed him was inevitable. But his thinking that I had been anything but completely into him burned viscerally. Everything I had done had been because of my feelings for him—because I didn't want to lose him. "Everything has not been a lie."

He stood up and started pacing. "This entire time, I thought you just liked spending time with me, that we were doing this project together because we cared about the musical. But you didn't care about the musical or me. You were just using me to win the competition."

"I was not using you."

"Then what were you doing?"

I didn't have an answer, and the longer I was silent, the more the silence became an answer. I wasn't using Wesley. I felt sure of that, but I didn't know how to explain what I had been doing, why I didn't tell him. I really didn't know what else to say at this point. Obviously he was going to twist whatever I said, so there was no point.

"Maybe I should go," I said. "Still have to pack for USF tomorrow."

Wesley nodded. "See you later."

I left as calmly as I could so that Mrs. Dixon wouldn't catch on to what had happened. Of course, that was assuming she hadn't heard us practically screaming at each other. If she had heard, she didn't let on. I got in my car, drove a little ways down the road to a lake that Wesley and I would visit sometimes. I parked away from the other cars and finally let myself cry.

17

— · —

The forty-five minute car ride to Tampa felt longer. I put in ear buds and attempted to blast my music loud enough to drown out my parents' conversation about USF, but every five minutes, Savannah would tap me on the shoulder to tell me that Mom was asking if I knew something about USF that was almost always common knowledge. It was going to be harder than I thought to pretend to be cheerful to be here.

I checked my phone probably about as often as Mom asked me a question, but Wesley still hadn't texted. Honestly, I didn't know what I was waiting for. Why on earth did I think he'd text me? We'd yelled, we'd said some things that were just hanging there between us, separating us. I had lied to him. I didn't know if we could ever get around those things again. And I didn't know what we would have if we couldn't. The thought that we might never get past it—never be what we were or what we had become—was sickening.

Once on campus, Dad parked in one of the bigger parking garages near the library. We had a scheduled tour planned, but Mom had insisted on getting there early so that we could have a look ourselves. I couldn't decide which would be better: a school-sanctioned tour with all their fake pushing of the school but silence from my mother, or a private family walk void of bureaucratic endorsements but filled with endless diatribes from my mother. Since I was somehow getting both, I guessed I would find out.

"Oh, look how pretty it is," Mom said, looking around. "The campus is even prettier than I remembered."

I shrugged. "Yeah, it's nice, I guess."

"You guess? Just look how many trees there are."

"Too many trees if you ask me." Who thought it was a good idea to plant so many oak trees so close together? One good hurricane, and they would have a lot of cleanup to do. What were they going to do in a few years when all those roots grew too close together? Spend tuition money to have the trees removed that they used tuition money to plant in the first place?

Mom said, "Let's pop into the library for a second. I really want to see it."

"All libraries are the same," I said, arms folded.

Dad beckoned me to follow. "There's a Starbucks inside. I'm buying."

My parents didn't often resort to bribery, but boy, did my dad know how to bribe me whenever he wanted. The promise of a Starbucks chai tea latte was enough to draw me in.

The library was big, as expected, and the Starbucks was drawing quite a crowd. Dad handed Savannah and me his credit card, gave us his and Mom's orders, and sent us off to procure caffeine, which would be absolutely necessary on this trip.

The line was long, and Savannah and I were getting a little antsy. I didn't drink coffee, but Savannah did, and she was definitely getting cranky without her fix. I kept trying to convince her that we were just minutes away from coffee, but she was acting playfully dramatic.

"We're gonna end up spending the entire day standing in this line," she said.

"Beats listening to Mom drone on about the school."

Savannah whipped her head around. "Are you going to be Squidward all day?"

"Squidward?"

"Yeah, you're all bitter and boring like Squidward."

"I am not bitter and boring."

"Prove it, then. At least try to have a little fun. Geez, you act like the president of USF killed a relative or something."

"I just don't want to be here."

"Yeah, I think we all got that."

"Fine, I'll try to fake it better. How's that?"

"Better."

We ordered, picked up our drinks, and found Dad, but Mom was nowhere to be seen.

Dad shrugged. "She ran off in that direction."

We followed her outside of the library where she was chatting with a student that appeared to be a tour guide since he was wearing a USF-branded polo and was carrying a tour group sign. He seemed cheerful enough, but Mom was talking his ear off for sure, so he had to be wearing out. Finally, she released him from her figurative clutches and waved her arm dramatically so we would join her.

"That was Enrique. He's one of the tour guides. He says there's a meet and greet later today for accepted students. You should go."

"Why?"

"Marjorie, to meet people," she said with an excess of enthusiasm. No one who ever met my mom would have been surprised to find out that she was a cheerleader in high school. "These could be potential classmates. Plus, he says some of the department heads and other professors attend those kinds of things. You could get to know some people in the political science department."

"But—"

"It can't hurt."

I looked to Savannah for help, but she just gave me two thumbs up, so I sighed. "Fine. I'll do it."

Mom clapped her hands excitedly, then threw her arm around my shoulder, leading me off to the rest of the campus.

*****

It was hot today, as was the norm in Florida, and all of the walking outside had caused all of us to work up a sweat, but Mom wouldn't be deterred so easily. She sent Dad on a few water runs but insisted that we keep "exploring" as she called it. Though I hadn't said it out loud, I had to admit that the campus was really pretty. I wasn't a big fan of the Tampa area, but USF was like its own little world in the middle of Tampa. The campus was well-designed, and even though we were tired and sweaty, we hadn't been walking for that long since the campus basically went in a circle. It was decent, I supposed.

We landed at the student center for Dad's latest water run, and Savannah and I managed to convince our mother to go inside the student center. We spun a story about wanting to see the inside, but really we just wanted the A/C.

For a school the size of USF, I half-expected the student center to be bigger, so the tall, skinny building seemed inadequately small, but once inside, it seemed massive compared to how it had appeared. The center of the building was open all the way up with the staircase wrapping the sides. There seemed to be a food court off to one side and a more common area to the other side. Dad came back with water bottles from the food court, raving about how there was a Papa John's and a Subway—his two favorite places.

"There's a Moe's, too," he said. "You could probably get a job pretty easily there."

I scoffed. "I'd like to get out of the Mexican fast food business, if possible."

"But it's decent money, and you already know the job."

I shrugged. "I suppose."

Actually, if I wanted, I could be profiting off of the nonprofit. Technically, I was owner and CEO, and I could be awarding myself a salary if I wanted. I hadn't done it at first because I was afraid we wouldn't be able to raise enough money, and I didn't want to siphon any out. Later, it felt selfish to take money from that when I didn't need it. I wondered what would happen to Spotlight Heroes once the competition was over.

"Also," Dad continued, "the cashier told me that there are two more Starbucks on this campus. Can you believe it? Three Starbucks on the whole campus. That's amazing."

I muttered something in agreement, but really I was distracted by the courtyard that was visible through the glass doors opposite the student center. Without realizing it, I drifted in that direction, and everyone else just kind of followed me.

Behind the student center was a big fountain with a bull statue—USF's mascot was the bull, and they were apparently obsessed with it—and beyond that was a walkway covered with arches and pink flowers. Once I got outside, I saw that the courtyard kept going toward the right with a big green lawn with zig-zagging walkways I saw the contemporary art museum and anticipated Dad's jokes about contemporary art looking like a kindergartener's mud sculpture, but I couldn't get over how pretty it all looked. I saw a few students studying on some benches under the flowered walkways and thought that that must be a fantastic place to study. USF may not be the right school for me, but no one could deny that the campus was beautiful.

As we walked the greens, and Mom and Dad flipped furiously through the many pamphlets they'd managed to obtain at the student center, I checked my phone. Still nothing.

"Stop obsessing," Savannah said. "It's creepy."

"Shut up."

"Here, take a picture of me quick while Mom and Dad are distracted."

"Why do they have to be distracted?"

"Do you want to be the one to start the picture-taking? Mom'll never stop."

I shrugged. "Fair enough. Stand over there by the tree."

Savannah smiled, I snapped a picture, then she struck a few silly poses, and I snapped again. When Mom turned to look at us, Savannah quickly spun around and pointed at the tree as if she was noticing something. I barely contained my urge to laugh. Once Mom became absorbed in the pamphlets again, Savannah jogged back over to me.

"Let me see."

I handed her my phone, and she flipped through, sending a few of her favorites to herself.

"Whoa, who are these old people?" she said, turning my phone so I could see. It was a picture from the Strawberry Festival.

"That's Barbara and Edward."

"Oh, Barbara and Edward, right, how could I not have known?"

I glared. "Wesley and I met them at the Festival. They offered to take a picture for us. They were really nice."

"You guys are so boring. Taking pictures with elderlies?"

"They were really sweet."

"So is that who you're waiting to hear from? The reason you keep checking your phone obsessively?"

"I doubt Barbara and Edward are big texters."

"You know what I mean." When I didn't answer, she asked, "So did you guys have a fight?"

"Why is that always your first guess?"

"Am I right this time?"

"We had an argument, yes."

"So call him."

"I can't."

"Why not?"

"I just can't."

Savannah huffed. "The two of you are impossible."

"Marjorie," Mom said as she and Dad walked back over to us. "The honors college is just up ahead. Should we take a look?"

"Honors college?"

I had wanted to do the honors program at UF, but now that everything there was in jeopardy, I didn't know how likely it was. I'd gotten into the honors college at USF already. Originally, I had no intentions of applying to anything at USF beyond general admission, but the application was really similar to UF's, so I basically had everything done for it, so I went ahead and submitted it.

I tried to shrug casually. "I guess it couldn't hurt."

18

—·—

I had barely agreed to go on this visit to USF—mostly to get my mom to stop talking about it and partly because I felt bad for snapping at her—but I definitely had not agreed to some cheesy meet and greet situation. Meet and greets were always the most awkward, forced things in the world. Why did anybody think that people actually wanted to attend meet and greets? Did extroverts like these? That was the only reasonable explanation.

To add to the awkwardness, it seemed that most of the admitted students here today were also introverts who got their arms twisted by their moms, so no one was willing to make the first move and initiate conversation. We all either stood or sat in separate parts of the room on our phones. It was definitely uncomfortable, but I could pass a couple of hours like this: I had seventy-six percent battery and a lot of games on my phone.

I knew what I would see, but I still checked my text messages anyway. Still nothing from Wesley. I did have a text from Taylor asking what had happened between us, but I didn't have the energy to type that reply right now. In fact, I wasn't even sure if I could type that. That was more of an in-person conversation.

And what had happened? I had insulted him; he had insulted me. We hadn't spoken since. Wesley and I had had fights, of course, but not like this, not this bad, not after we had *kissed*. I didn't know what would happen at this point.

One of the USF students who had organized this event decided singlehandedly to get everyone talking. "Okay, everyone," she said with a cheery voice and a single clap of her hands, "we're going to play an icebreaker."

I think the worst word in the entire English language was just that: icebreaker.

"Find a buddy, then ask each other three questions each. Nothing serious, just silly questions. If you don't have anything in common, move on to someone new. If you do, then you just made a new friend."

Why were these things always like this? Who enjoyed this? I thought about giving the most obscure answers possible so that no one would agree. Of course, I might find that one weirdo dude who actually liked freaky stuff. Or I could end up talking to a lot of people. Maybe I should say something really generic like my favorite movie is *Mean Girls,* just to end the misery.

Refusing to participate, I did not move from my seat. If it came down to it, I could pretend to get a phone call or pass out or something. Anything would be better.

There was a girl sitting a few seats down from me also poking around on her phone. Either she was actually texting someone or she was way better at faking it than I was. Unfortunately, she caught me staring at her, and I tried to look away, but it was definitely too late.

"Hate these things," she muttered. "If I wanted to talk, I would."

I laughed. "Exactly."

She spun around in her seat to face me. "Right? Like, I'm eighteen years old. I know how to put full sentences together and say them to another person. I don't need a school sanctioned event to do it."

We both laughed. At least if I was stuck here, I found someone whom I didn't absolutely hate. She wiped the tears from laughing from her eyes and smiled. "I'm Lana."

"Jorie."

"Jorie?"

"My full name is Marjorie, but I don't really like it, so I go by Jorie."

She nodded. "I like that. It's original. I'll probably never meet another Jorie."

"Yeah, well you might not meet a Marjorie either unless it's like a grandma or something."

She snickered. She was really pretty. Her hair was long and dark, nearly black, and she wore this really interesting purple eyeliner. She propped her arm up on the back of the chair and smiled. She just exuded confidence. Her smile was infectious. If I did go to USF, I imagined that we could have been friends.

"Okay, okay," she said. "Let's find something in common so that they don't make us talk to more people. Where are you from?"

"Here."

She looked around the room. "I like it, but personally, way too much green and gold."

I laughed again. "I meant Florida. I live a little less than an hour away."

"I'm from Hawaii."

"That's so cool. I've always wanted to go there."

"It's gorgeous, for sure, but highly overrated. People always ask me, 'why would you go to school in Florida when you live in Hawaii?' but I'm tired of it, you know? Plus, I like Tampa."

I couldn't help but snicker. "I didn't think anybody really liked Tampa."

"It's so eclectic. Where I live, everyone is the same. It's a pretty small town, close-knit community. It's either native Hawaiians or people with Japanese heritage like me." Japanese—that's what it was. I couldn't place something about the look of her face. "I'm just tired of the small town life, I guess. In Tampa, there are people from all over."

"I guess that's true," I said, though I wasn't sure I could relate. I didn't hate River Glen just because it was small. Sometimes I didn't like River Glen and wanted to leave, but it was home. "So you're set on USF?"

She nodded. "I accepted the day I got the letter. It is my dream school."

"That's great."

"I take it you haven't accepted?"

I shook my head. "Hoping to get off the waitlist somewhere else."

"That's too bad. We could've been roommates and never spoken to each other. Okay, you ask the next question."

"Major?"

"Speech language pathology."

"What is that?"

"Basically, it's studying communication and speech disorders and different types of speech. My brother is Deaf. That's kind of how I got into it. I might double major with Deaf studies. We'll see."

"That's so cool. I don't think I've ever heard of a Deaf studies major before."

She shrugged and smiled. "It's not something you can get anywhere, but it's really interesting, and USF has a really cool Deaf studies program. That's actually how I found out about USF. Okay, your turn. Major?"

"I was thinking of double majoring, too. I'll major in political science, but I've thought about adding business or criminal justice. I'll be pre-law."

"Ooh, a lawyer. That's sick."

Lana was so easy to talk to. It was like we'd been friends for years, like she's someone I would have hung out with on the weekends with Taylor and Wesley. In fact, I was certain that if we had gone to school together that we would have been friends. At least in the middle of this crappy event, I had found someone I could stand.

I said, "We still haven't found something in common."

"Whoops," she said with a laugh. "Okay, here's a weird one."

"Why ask a weird one? We'll never agree."

"You never know. This was an application essay question, I think. If you could have dinner with any president, which one would you choose?"

"Andrew Jackson."

"For real?"

"No doubt. He's so weird and controversial. I feel like he'd be fun to have a conversation with."

"Totally."

"Wait, did you—"

Lana nodded. "He's by far the most interesting president. He just did whatever he wanted and didn't care what anybody else thought."

We both laughed. "If nothing else, dinner with him would be hilarious."

"For sure."

The USF student walked over and put her hands on her hips. "Looks like we've found some new friends."

"Eh," Lana said with a shrug, "we'll see. Jury's still out on this one."

I laughed, but the USF chick definitely didn't get Lana's humor. She smiled awkwardly and excused herself, causing Lana and me to devolve into a fit of giggles.

"Oh man, Jorie, you should pick USF so that we can keep terrorizing these cheery people."

***

Later on, I had a meeting with the political science department head and a few professors. The department head was this older woman who seemed very kind. She took the time to chat individually with each of the political science majors in the room, and even though that wasn't a lot of people, it was still really nice of her to do.

I wished Lana was majoring in political science so that she would be here. It was a lot more fun talking to her than sitting here in this room of like four guys.

I had already spoken to the head Dr. Setton, so I wasn't really sure what else I was supposed to be doing here. I was pretty much just watching people talk to Dr. Setton, and I was starting to wonder if anyone would notice if I just left. Just as I was plotting my escape, I noticed a professor sitting off to the side, and his name tag said that he was involved in business as well as politics and law. I decided that it couldn't hurt to talk to him. Make connections, right? That's what the guidance counselor always said.

The only problem: I didn't know how to strike up a conversation with a total stranger. I realized that was the whole point of this dumb thing, but how do you do it? What was the right opener for a random intrusion into someone's career and education?

I sat down next to him, leaving a chair in between us so I didn't look weird, and forced out, "Do you mind if I sit here?"

"Not at all," he said with a smile. "It's a little awkward just sitting here, isn't it?" He was middle-aged and couldn't look more like a typical professor. He was wearing really nice jeans and an Oxford jacket, and his beard that was little more than a scruff and black frame glasses completed the look.

I nodded. "Just a little."

He jutted out his hand for a handshake. "I'm Dr. Jameson."

"Jorie."

"Are you from around here, Jorie?"

"Yeah, I live a little over an hour away."

"That's great. Going to school so close to home definitely has its perks."

"I actually haven't decided if I'm going here yet. I was accepted, but I'm still waiting to hear from some other schools."

He nodded. "That's fair. So, why do you want to major in political science?"

"I'm going to be a lawyer."

"Love the confidence. I went to law school, too, but I didn't like practicing all that much. I preferred teaching. Do you want to practice?" When I nodded, he added, "What kind of law?"

"I'm not really sure yet. I want to do something that will really make a difference. Something that will benefit kids or schools or something like that."

"A noble goal. We need more lawyers like that, and all the better to get more female lawyers like that. So how's senior year? Anything interesting going on?"

I couldn't really think of anything interesting going on with me—I was pretty sure Dr. Jameson didn't want to hear about my drama with

Wesley, and I definitely didn't want to tell him—so I decided to tell him about the project. If anyone was going to listen to my ideas, it would be him. Who knows? Maybe he'd be able to offer some advice or something. At least that way I could do something productive and useful instead of just destroying everything. I explained the competition and my project with Wesley, and he seemed genuinely interested.

"That's so fascinating," he said. "And it worked? The musical's fully funded?"

I nodded. "I mean, we're still waiting to hear from a couple of donors, but I'm pretty sure they'll come through."

"That's insane. I love seeing that kind of initiative from the next generation. So what's next?"

"Next?"

"For the business. I hope you're not stopping here."

"Well, I actually was thinking about expanding. I'd love to benefit theater in more than just my school."

"Are you thinking other schools?"

"Yes, and community theater, kids clubs, stuff like that. Really, any kind of theater for kids that needs the support. I don't know if that's going to happen though."

"Why not?"

Because I wasn't sure if Wesley would ever speak to me again. "I'm not sure of my college plans yet, so I'm not sure if I'll continue with it."

"Well, I certainly hope you do. That could be a really cool project for a seminar or capstone class. That's the kind of project I'd love to mentor. I have an MBA too, you know. I got it after law school when I realized I didn't want to practice. This is the kind of thing I'd love to work on."

"Really?"

"Definitely. I know you're undecided about USF, but if you haven't already, you should definitely let the department know about this. It could earn you a scholarship if you're lucky."

"I didn't think it mattered since I was already accepted."

"Oh, it definitely matters. The department loves stuff like this. I'm not saying a scholarship is a guarantee, but it's definitely a possibility."

"Okay," I said. I guessed applying for a scholarship couldn't hurt.

"And I know you're still undecided, but I hope you'll seriously consider USF. This is a great place to be to pursue multiple interests, and if your nonprofit becomes something that you intend to pursue long-term, I would be more than happy to offer any assistance I could. That's a very exciting project. Good luck with the competition. I hope you win."

"Thank you," I said, and Dr. Jameson moved on to the guy wearing a suit next to me. Who wears a suit to a casual meet and greet?

If nothing else, it was cool to meet Dr. Jameson. Other than Ms. Corwin and maybe Evan, I hadn't seen anyone else get that excited about this project, and he was the first to agree with me about expansion. I couldn't help but wonder if he would still be willing to help me if I attended UF. Would it matter if I wasn't his student?

The worst of the meet and greet was over, so I headed back to the main room where Lana and I had agreed to meet up after our department meetings. There was still a lot of uncertainty in my life, but I felt just a little less heavy after my conversation with Dr. Jameson.

Lana and I exchanged phone numbers, promising to keep in touch even if we weren't going to be at the same school, and I headed back to the student center where my family was waiting. As soon as they saw me, Mom and Dad started peppering me with questions about the meet and greet, the department meeting, whether I had made any friends, did I hear about any classes I liked, what was the building like, and so on. My dad even asked if they had served cookies and was pleased with the answer that Publix chocolate chip cookies had, in fact, been served.

After a few minutes, Savannah sighed loudly and dramatically. "Okay, well some of us did not eat Publix cookies and are therefore starving."

"We ate, like, two hours ago," I said.

"Well that's two hours since I've eaten."

"You're so dramatic."

"Oh yeah, because *I'm* the dramatic one in this family."

Dad held up his hands between us and said, "I'll take Savannah to the food court. I've been eyeing that Subway since we got here. Marjorie, I take it you're not hungry?"

I shook my head.

Mom said, "I'm not really either, so you two go ahead. Marjorie and I will take a seat over there and chat until you get back."

Savannah and Dad made a beeline for the Subway, and Mom led me to a couch down one of the hallways. It was a little more secluded down here and much less plagued by the din of the main area of the student center. I wasn't sure if Mom actually wasn't hungry or not, but I knew her real motivation was asking what I thought about USF.

As if on cue, as soon as we sat down, she said, "So how was it?"

I shrugged. "Okay, I guess."

"Okay? That's all I get?"

"Mom." I rolled my eyes. "It was a meet and greet. How do you think it went?"

"I know you hate that kind of stuff, but wasn't there anything interesting?"

"There was this one girl, Lana. She was pretty cool."

"That's exciting."

"And one of the poly sci professors was kind of interesting."

"How so?"

I fidgeted with the hem of my shirt. I hadn't really talked much about the project to my parents, or Savannah for that matter, since Wesley and I first got it off the ground. They didn't know a lot of what had happened behind the scenes. I didn't know how she'd react, but I felt an I-told-you-so hanging in the air somewhere.

"Well, he's got a J.D., but he's not a lawyer. Like, he doesn't practice."

"A J.D. doesn't automatically make you a lawyer."

"Yeah, I know, but he also has an MBA."

Mom chuckled. "Oh Marjorie, always looking for a way to multi-task. You know, one degree would be just fine."

I pointed a finger. "But there's nothing wrong with getting two."

She laughed again. "Certainly not. So he's in business?"

"No, he's just a professor, but he teaches all the law and business related classes. He was interested in Spotlight Heroes."

"You told him about that?"

I nodded. "He says I should apply for a scholarship because of it."

"You absolutely should."

"And that if I went to USF, he'd love to mentor me and help with the project."

She clasped her hands together. "Ooh, that's so exciting."

I shrugged. "I guess."

"Sounds like it wasn't all bad."

"No," I said reluctantly, "it's not all bad. But may I remind you that I never said it was."

"Fair enough, but I knew there was something for you here. I could just sense it."

"You could not."

She nodded emphatically. "Mothers can sense these things. If your brain weren't filled with a million tiny little stop signs, you might have sensed it, too."

I couldn't help but laugh out loud, drawing the attention of some students nearby. "A million tiny little stop signs?"

"Yes."

"Oh my gosh."

"So would you do it?"

"What?"

She let out a small huff. "If you picked USF, would you take him up on his offer of a mentorship?"

"That's a big if."

"Humor me."

I avoided eye contact. "Maybe. I don't know."

"Why not?"

I pulled a loose thread out of the hem of my shirt, then pulled a thread that wasn't so loose. "I don't know what I'm going to do with Spotlight Heroes."

"Is everything okay?"

I felt a stinging in the back of my throat, and my eyes burned a little, but I was determined not to cry. "Everything's fine."

Mom stayed quiet for a few moments, probably sensing what was happening. How do moms always know when you're upset no matter how good you are at hiding it?

After a little while, she said, "You know, there are some pretty cool stores in the area. I was thinking before we head over to UT that we might do a little shopping. You still haven't picked a prom dress."

The burning and the stinging intensified at the mention of prom. Who knew if Wesley even still wanted to go to prom with me.

I blinked several times in a desperate attempt to will the tears to stay inside my head, but I was slowly losing the battle. I sniffed louder than I had intended, and Mom slipped an arm around me. "Honey, is something wrong?"

The battle was finally lost, and tears slipped quickly down my cheeks. I tried to hold in the sobs, but it seemed that the more I tried to hold them in, the more determined they became to force their way out. I started ugly crying right there in the middle of the USF student center, and it was mortifying, but I didn't know how to make it stop. Mom forced me to stand and ushered me outside to a park bench where I cried for what could have been two minutes or half an hour, I couldn't be sure.

When I finally slowed down and regained some control, Mom rubbed my back and said, "Tell me what happened."

I sniffed loudly. "I don't know. I think I messed everything up."

"Messed what up?"

"Everything with Wesley."

"Do you mean the project?"

I flung my arms up with minimal effort, and they flopped back down. "The project and everything else. I lied to him over and over, and he just kept taking it, and then I said terrible things to him, and he said terrible things, too, and I don't even know if we're going to prom anymore, much less if we're even still friends."

"Oh, you and Wesley have been best friends for too long for a fight to end that."

Another sniff. "You didn't hear the fight."

"Maybe not, but Wesley has a good heart. I'm sure you two can find your way back to each other. This project will be over soon, and then things can go back to normal."

"It's not just the project."

"Then what else?"

I swallowed hard. "I never told you, but we kind of had a thing at the Strawberry Festival, and—"

"A fight kind of thing?"

"No." When my mother looked confused, I added, "A different kind of thing."

She nodded slowly. "Oh."

"And I liked it, Mom. I think I might even love him, but now he's never going to speak to me again, and all because I didn't get into UF and instead of telling him, I used him to try to get in anyway."

She looked genuinely surprised. "You didn't get into UF?"

"I thought maybe Savannah told you."

She shook her head. "How long have you known?"

"Weeks. I did the project because I was hoping to get off the waitlist. I don't even know if that's going to work, and now this random professor at USF is interested in the nonprofit, and I don't know what to do about that or Wesley or anything at this point."

Mom squeezed my shoulder and didn't speak again for a little while. I had no idea what she was thinking—was she mad, upset, worried, happy, prideful, afraid?—and I really wished I did know what was on her mind. I was still really upset about everything, and I still didn't have any answers, but somehow saying all of it out loud made it hurt just a tiny bit less.

Finally, Mom said, "I can't tell you what to do about UF, USF, or even Wesley, because you need to make those decisions on your own. Pick the school that makes you happy, that helps you achieve your goals, or define your goals if they've changed, and trust that if you and Wesley are meant to find your way back to each other, either as friends or as more, that you will. What I do know is that it sounds like you need to talk to him."

I nodded slowly. "I know. I just don't know what to say."

"Be honest with him. He might still be upset at first, but he deserves the truth from you before he makes any decisions." I nodded again. I desperately wanted to text him right then or call him, but I knew that this was a conversation better saved for in person. "And right now, I think that what you really need is frozen yogurt."

A chuckle escaped my lips. "Frozen yogurt doesn't fix everything."

"You don't know that until you try. Besides, USF's student center has a frozen yogurt machine. Does UF even have that?"

Another chuckle. "You don't ever give up, do you, Mom?"

She shook her head. "And neither should you. On anything."

19

As soon as we got home from Tampa, I dumped my bag in my room, hopped in my car, and drove to Wesley's house. Even if this ended in another fight, I had to talk to Wesley. I couldn't stand not talking any longer. I thought I could do this without him. I thought I would be fine with doing things on my own without Wesley's help. But I didn't necessarily need Wesley's help: I needed Wesley. Full stop. I'd been the one to push him away, and I hated myself for it now. I could only hope that there was some way I could salvage a relationship now. I knew that I wanted it to be more than a friendship, but any relationship where Wesley and I were on speaking terms was desirable at this point.

It was as if no time had passed at the Dixon house. When I pulled up, everything was exactly as it had been a couple of days ago. Wesley's dad was working on his car, and his mom greeted me at the door with a big smile to tell me that Wesley was in the den. How serendipitous it was that we should attempt to make up in the same room where we nearly lost each other.

I could only hope that Wesley felt the same way.

As before, I paused outside the French doors for a moment and just watched Wesley. He had both feet propped up on an ottoman and one arm across the back of the couch. It looked like he was reading something. He looked fairly relaxed, though, of course, he didn't know I was there. After Wesley and I had kissed, I eagerly awaited his reaction whenever he saw me because I had thought it would tell me something about how he was feeling. Instead, I had missed it entirely and was still confused. I hoped it would be different this time.

I knocked once, then opened the doors, and he didn't turn around right away. Did he already know? Had he somehow seen my car pull up? When he slipped a receipt into the book as a bookmark but didn't close the book immediately, I realized he was just finishing the page and breathed a sigh of relief.

When he turned around, his expression was utterly unreadable. He definitely didn't look mad, but he didn't exactly look happy either, and I couldn't decide if this indifference was a good thing or not.

"Jorie," he said, sounding surprised. "I didn't know you had gotten back."

I nodded. "Just a little while ago."

He set the book on the coffee table and gestured to the couch next to him, so I sat somewhat hesitatingly. "So how was it?"

"Pretty good. Not as bad as I thought it would be."

"Your mom must be thrilled, then."

I couldn't stop the smile that spread across my face. A joke. Wesley made a joke. "Ecstatic. She's practically paying the tuition as we speak."

He laughed, but it didn't sound totally free like Wesley normally sounded when he laughed. Still, he had made a joke. "I heard from another donor while you were gone. Gibson's Car Wash is pledging the full $500."

"That's fantastic. Only two more donors to hear from, then."

"Yep."

I fidgeted a little. "So how's the car? I didn't see it in the driveway."

"Good," he said. "It's actually in the shop right now getting fixed. I guess you won't have to pick me up anymore."

"You know I didn't mind."

"I know."

I desperately wanted to get this conversation started, but I didn't know how. It seemed too abrupt to shift from talking about car washes to *that*, but I didn't know how to make a transition. It seemed that every time I worked up the nerve to say something, he asked some mundane question that didn't matter. Before I could spit out what I wanted to say, Wesley spoke again.

"I'm sorry."

I shifted back into the couch a little. "For what?" I was the one who needed to apologize. I was the one who had treated Wesley like he meant nothing to me. And somehow knowing that it was all my fault made me feel even worse that he thought he had any reason to apologize.

"For being a jerk about UF and the project. I know how important UF is to you, and I shouldn't have overreacted."

"You didn't overreact. You were right to be mad."

"If I'm being honest—"

"Please do."

"—I'm still a little upset. I wish you had just told me. I would've understood."

"I know." I instinctively touched his arm then wondered if that was a mistake based on the way he looked over at my hand on his forearm. "I wanted to tell you a million times, but I thought you'd quit the project or be mad or—or not want to be around me anymore."

He chuckled a little. "Part of the reason I was hurt was because I wanted to be around you. I thought we were having fun together."

"We were."

"Were we? Or was it just the project?" He followed up quickly with, "Be honest."

"You're my best friend, so I'm never upset to be around you, but at first, I guess it was just about the project. But the more time we spent together, the more I became afraid of losing you, and it reached a point where it felt like it was too late to say anything."

He nodded. "I guess I can see that."

"The last thing I wanted was to hurt you."

"Same."

Neither of us spoke for a few minutes, and we mostly avoided eye contact. I knew we had to talk through some stuff, but I was afraid to bring it up, and it seemed like he was, too. Wesley was really outgoing most of the time, but I also knew that he could shut down if he didn't know what to say, so I decided this time I would make the first move.

"We should talk about the project," I said.

"Yeah."

"Do you still want to do it?"

Wesley didn't answer for longer than I wanted, but finally, he said, "We should finish it."

"Yeah?"

"Yeah. We've already done this much work. We should finish it. Besides, we can't just give up. Mr. King and the cast members are counting on us."

"Well we could finish the fundraising and not actually submit the project."

He seemed to consider this, but said, "No, let's see it through."

"Are you sure?"

"Yes."

"Okay, then we'll finish it as is."

"I think we should also still go to prom," he said, seeming to rush all the words together. "If you want to, of course."

"I would love to."

He smiled. "I was hoping you would say that."

"Me, too."

"I would never want to lose our friendship."

My heart sank a little at the word "friendship." "Same here."

He leaned forward for a quick hug, and I gladly accepted it, but he pulled away a little too soon, and I wanted to say something more, anything, but instead I smiled and said I was glad that we were still friends.

***

Spring break passed quickly, and Monday morning, we were back at school. Wesley and I had met up a few times over the break to finalize the project. It was mostly done at this point. We had a few final things we would add once the musical was over, but for now, we were pretty much done with the project. The only thing we had been waiting for was the final donors to come through, which they had, and for the IRS to state that our nonprofit application had been officially approved. Conveniently, I had just received that email over the weekend.

I wanted to call Wesley as soon as I got the letter, but I still didn't really know where we stood. We were friends again, and for the most part, we'd been back to normal, but Wesley had so clearly defined our relationship as a friendship. Sure, we were going to prom together, but what did that mean?

Perhaps I had been right all along, that dating your best friend was a mistake destined to end in pain. Maybe it was better that it ended now, before it got too serious, before it was too late for our friendship to resurrect and survive the damage. Still, that didn't ease the ache I felt in my chest every time he smiled or laughed, and I desperately wanted to kiss him.

Mr. King had called another meeting before school, and I assumed it was to tell the cast that everything was set to go. Most people already knew since Wesley and I had kept everyone up to date, but this was an opportunity for Mr. King to be dramatic and theatrical, and he never passed up that kind of opportunity.

I got there early, as I assumed Wesley would, and met Mr. King in the cafeteria. Wesley was already there chatting with Mr. King, each of them with their legs propped up in the edge of the steps. That ache in my chest made its reappearance at the sight of him.

"Miss Haywood," Mr. King said, jumping out of his chair and spreading his arms, "it is a joy and a delight to see you."

"Uh, thanks, Mr. King."

"Mr. Dixon says you have our final numbers?"

I handed him the folder. "Everything is in there. You should receive a check from the last donor today."

"Exquisite," he said, poring over the details of spreadsheets.

I walked over to Wesley, and he smiled and waved.

"You know," he said, "he didn't say it was a joy and a delight to see me. I think I'm insulted."

I let out a small chuckle. "I wouldn't be too offended if I were you. Do you really want him to say that to you?"

He shrugged. "Fair enough."

"So, I have a surprise for you."

"What's that?"

I slammed the printed email from the IRS onto the step next to him. He looked surprised, but he picked it up and scanned.

His eyes darted up to meet mine. "It's official?"

I smiled. "It's official."

"That's fantastic. Man, just in the nick of time, too."

"I know, right?"

"So all we need to do now is write up the extra part of the presentation that relates to this?"

I slammed another paper down next to him. "Already done."

"You're on fire."

I sat down on the step next to him. "So what are the chances that Mr. King is going to embarrass us in front of the entire cast?"

"Oh, 100%."

As if on cue, the rest of the cast started trickling in. It was obvious that everyone knew why we'd been called here today. We'd continued rehearsals as soon as Wesley and I met the first fundraising goal, but there was still this bulging tension at every rehearsal as people wondered whether all the hard work would actually culminate in something.

I was so glad that it was actually happening. Rachel was going to be beautiful in that gold dress as Belle, and she was going to charm the entire crowd. I made a mental note to visit next year to see her in whatever musical Mr. King chose. I knew she'd shine in just about any role, and it would so interesting to see a production that didn't have Sienna in it. Drew and Wesley were going to win over everyone with their performances, and the supporting cast was funny, talented, and genuinely incredible. After everything that had happened, I was surprised to find myself thinking that this might end up being the best production I'd been a part of.

Mr. King waved his arms wildly above his head until everyone started to settle, at which point he silenced us with a conductor's cue. "My fellow thespians, I stand before you a proud man, a man of exceedingly good fortune, a fortune the mighty Macbeth could have only dreamed of." I knew one thing for sure: I was going to miss Mr. King's dramatic speeches. "It is with a fervent heart that I announce that the musical is officially saved. Our powerful Gaston and illustrious stage director have performed the impossible and pulled *Beauty and the Beast* from the pit in which it had found itself."

Sienna said, "So the donors finally coughed up some cash?"

Mr. King huffed a quick sigh. "The donors were persuaded by the incomparable efforts of Miss Haywood and Mr. Dixon. Without them, this musical would not be happening. Let us raise our hands in a round of applause for our Spotlight Heroes."

The cast—excluding Sienna, of course—applauded heartily, and, strangely, I found myself getting emotional at Mr. King's reference to us as the spotlight heroes. I had named the organization because of the impact I saw Rachel having. I didn't think the term applied to me. I caught myself wondering if there was any way I could continue this work, stay close to the school and the theater, continue to be a part of this experience.

It's rare in life to recognize in the moment that you will remember something forever without needing hindsight to recognize its value, and this was one of those moments. I had loved high school, and even though I was greatly looking forward to college, I wasn't necessarily eager to graduate. River Glen Academy had been home, and in this moment, I realized just how much I didn't want to leave home.

20

"Would you sit still?" Savannah insisted, pressing my shoulder down to force me back into the chair. She was attempting to curl my hair, but, as usual, it wasn't going well.

"I have to be close to the mirror to do eyeliner," I said.

"Well, then wait to do your eyeliner."

"Then hurry up with my hair."

"Hey, I'm trying to make your lifeless hair actually do something. It takes effort. And time. Now sit still."

I shifted back and held my head up. "So bossy."

I usually hated having my hair curled because it brought back memories of cotillion classes and elderly women commenting about how I looked like the perfect Southern belle, and there was nothing I hated more. But Savannah had some kind of magic ability to curl my hair and make it look good, not like a '50s country music star.

"Should I brush out your curls or leave them tight?"

"Leave them tight," I said. "If you brush them out, my hair will be totally straight by the time we arrive."

"I'm so glad you got the navy dress in the end. It's going to look so good with your hair."

"That was my argument for the green. Redheads look best in green."

Savannah let a curl fall, then, deciding it wasn't right, redid it. "Only the right shade of green. That was the wrong shade of green. Besides, it's your senior prom. You should look like a Hollywood movie star."

I snorted. "If you say so."

***

I smoothed the lines of my dress and reluctantly admitted to myself that Savannah was right: the navy dress was the right call. I'd loved the shape of it when I saw it in the store—it was a trumpet style with a high neckline, lower back, and sleeveless—but I was afraid that the color would be too boring. I was definitely wrong about that.

I reached for a bracelet sitting on my dresser, and my eyes landed on the boutonniere that I had bought for Wesley. We'd coordinated so that his boutonniere and my corsage would match: white roses with a navy ribbon. Looking at it now, I could picture myself pinning it on his lapel. We'd done it before. When we went to homecoming together sophomore year, we almost didn't buy them, but our mothers insisted that it was part of the process. I couldn't pin the stupid thing to save my life. Eventually, his mom had to do it. He had stupidly bought the kind of corsage that you pin to a dress, not slip on the wrist. Jokingly, I pinned it to the center of my dress. My mother scolded me and pinned it to a hair tie so I could put it on my wrist. It was so simple then. We were just playing around, having a good time without any expectations. I had a feeling it wouldn't be that way this time.

I put on the wine colored lipstick that Savannah insisted I wear and tried not to freak out when I heard the doorbell. I heard Wesley talking to my mom, who was already laughing. Wesley really was capable of charming anyone, including parents. My mom had always liked him, but ever since my meltdown at USF, she'd been really friendly with him any time she saw him. I think she was probably hoping that we would get back together—or, really, together for the first time—because she probably thought it would make me want to go to USF to stay near him. I definitely wasn't going to pick a school based on a guy, even if that guy was Wesley, but I'd be lying if I said it wasn't a factor.

"Marjorie," my mom called out with a sing-song voice, "Wesley is here."

I took one last look in the mirror, took a deep breath, and prepared to go down the stairs. We were friends. Good friends. Best friends. We would have a fantastic time at prom together because we were best friends. We were going to ride in a limo with Drew, Rachel, Taylor, and her boyfriend Ethan, dance to music, eat moderately funky food, and go to the beach afterward. It would be a lot of fun. I'd remember this night for the rest of my life.

But I wouldn't kiss Wesley.

I walked out of my room, Savannah gave me a wolf whistle, and I turned the corner to the stairs. Walking down stairs in a trumpet dress and heels was definitely complicated, but I resolved myself not to trip. Once I was far enough down the stairs to see my mom, dad, and Wesley, my cotillion training kicked in, and I smiled because I knew my mother would have the camera ready.

The flashes from the camera were a little blinding, but not blinding enough for me to miss the look on Wesley's face. He smiled, but he looked a little surprised, and I didn't miss the quick up and down glance he made at my dress.

Best friends didn't look at best friends like that.

He was wearing a navy suit with a white shirt and matching navy tie. Combined with his black wavy hair, he looked more suave than I had ever seen him, the real suave, not the fake suave he put on as Gaston.

A few girls in the junior class came to mind because I knew they'd be staring at him.

Was I jealous?

"Okay, you two," Mom said, waving her arms at us, "get close. Smile so I can take a picture."

Wesley slowly put an arm around my waist, but he only made as much contact as necessary to take the picture. Was that because we truly were just friends, or because my dad was watching?

"Wait, the lighting is bad," Mom said. "Scooch over there."

We shuffled back and forth around the entire living room as my mother searched for the perfect light. She finally found it near the same painting where we take literally all of our important pictures. I didn't know why she tried anywhere else. One time, Savannah complained that we never take pictures anywhere else, so my mom swore off that location for months, but she hated every picture we took other places, so back to the painting we went.

Mom tried to zoom in, and the entire system fell apart as Dad attempted to help her zoom back out, so Wesley and I ended up just standing there for a while, waiting for them to figure out their cell phone cameras. I was acutely aware of the fact that Wesley hadn't removed his arm from my waist.

"We're going to be here all night at this rate," I said.

He laughed. "Probably."

"Oh, by the way, I wrote up the interviews with the cast members. Once the musical is over, I'll do the write—"

"Nope, no project talk tonight. Tonight we just have fun."

"Deal."

"By the way, uh, you look beautiful."

My face felt hot. "Thank you. You look great, too."

***

The limo ride to the dinner cruise where prom was being held was, as expected, a total blast. We all sang along to every song as loudly as we possibly could. Our limo driver could probably hear us through the partition and hated us for it. After a scary, steep climb up the steps onto the dinner cruise ship, we ate a surprisingly delicious dinner and hit the dance floor, which was on an upper level of the ship.

As kids who all grew up in the country in the middle of nowhere who had attended private school for most of our lives, most of us had no idea how to dance outside of line dances and whatever dance they taught at cotillion. Dancing at prom was always more of a group huddle of everyone singing along and vaguely jumping or swaying to the beat. So when Wesley asked me to dance during Lee Brice's 'I Don't Dance" which happened to be my favorite song in the world, I was very surprised.

We both automatically defaulted to formal cotillion poses, but it just felt so wrong that we both laughed and shifted. He put his hands on my waist, and I looped mine over his shoulders, linking my fingers behind his neck to avoid running my hands through his hair. I assumed he picked this song to dance to because he knew I loved it.

But best friends didn't slow dance to romantic songs.

"Good night?" he asked.

I nodded. "Perfect night."

"Perfect?" he asked with a raised eyebrow. He almost seemed disappointed by that answer.

"The food was good, the music is good, we have great friends." Did I dare? "I'm with you. What more do I need?"

Wesley smiled, but still, that look of disappointment seemed to worm its way back onto his face though he seemed to be trying to fight it.

"What is it?" I asked. He shook his head, but I pressed him.

"I'm confused."

"By what?"

"By you."

"I'm not confusing."

He nodded. "You are. One minute, I'm sure you want—I don't know, something more. But the next minute, you're talking about us as friends. I never know what to do."

"*You* never know what to do? *I* never know what to do. You're the confusing one."

"I am not."

"You're the one who shut down any talk of us being more."

"*You* did that."

"When?"

"After you got back from USF," he said. "I told you that I wanted to spend time with you, and you said we were best friends."

"Well, aren't we?"

"You're so stubborn."

I scoffed. "Well, what about you? You said we shouldn't fight because you didn't want to lose our friendship."

"Because you had already said we were friends."

"I was trying to apologize for being a jerk."

"It sounded like you were telling me you just wanted to be friends."

I had to chuckle. "Why do you think I'm always friend zoning you?"

"Because you always are."

I rested my forehead on his shoulder and just started laughing. It was totally the wrong time to be laughing, but I couldn't help it. It was truly amazing how dysfunctional we had been. "Why are we so bad at this?"

"We're both trying too hard to avoid actually saying something."

"Well, I don't want to be wrong."

"Neither do I."

Wesley smiled, and I felt his hands tighten a little on my waist. "Jorie, I like you. I've liked you for several years now, but I didn't know how to say it or if I even should. I want to be more than just friends."

"Really?"

He rolled his eyes and shifted his hands up to my back and kissed me, finally kissed me after weeks of fighting and awkwardness. It felt just as good as the kiss on the Ferris wheel. No, better, because everything was clear this time.

Mr. Quentin cleared his throat as he walked past us, so Wesley pulled back and smirked, sending me into fits of laughter. A lot of people around us were definitely staring, and I suddenly became aware of the fact that we might have been kind of loud arguing with each other, but Lee Brice was still pounding in my ears, and I could still feel Wesley's lips on mine, so I gleefully ignored them.

Suddenly, Wesley started laughing, outright laughing loudly and strongly. I asked him why he was laughing, but it took him a minute to compose himself before he could answer.

"I just can't believe what a cliché I am."

"What do you mean?" I asked.

"I kissed you on a Ferris wheel, I asked you to prom with chocolate covered strawberries, and now I'm kissing you at prom while we're dancing to your favorite love song. We even got scolded by the principal."

I started laughing now, too. "You are a cliché."

"I can't believe it. My younger self would be so mad at me for being such a dork."

"Taylor is never going to let me live this down."

"So, what do you think? Do you still want to be with me even if I'm a cheesy rom-com cliché?"

I gently touched the side of his face. "Always."

21

—·—

"Stop fidgeting," I told Rachel. She hadn't stopped shifting back and forth or fiddling with her costume or props for about ten minutes now. "You're going to be fantastic."

"I'm just so nervous," she said. "I feel like there's so much anticipation for this now. What if I mess it up?"

I put a hand on each of her shoulders. "You will not mess it up. You're perfect for this role. Even if you make a mistake, it's a lighthearted Disney musical. Just roll with it." She nodded and swallowed hard. "I promise it'll be great."

Rachel was about to say something when we heard a crash. We peeked around the corner to see that Sienna had accidentally hit Jamar with the spout of her teapot costume.

"Hey," Jamar said as he regained his balance, "watch it, will you?"

"Ugh, this thing is so annoying," Sienna said.

I leaned closer to Rachel. "If anybody messes this up, it might be Sienna knocking someone unconscious with that thing."

That sent Rachel into a fit of giggles, and it seemed like she would be all right.

The curtain would be going up in just a couple of minutes, so I double-checked that all of the sets and props were in the right place and then reapplied my lipstick. This ridiculous fluffy dress did not make moving sets easy, but I still had to make sure that everything would run smoothly during the show.

Wesley walked over and asked me to spray his hair with hairspray. He'd managed to convince Mr. King not to make him wear a wig since his own hair is naturally black and thick, but it still required a lot of hairspray and gel to get it to have the appropriate volume befitting Gaston. I doused him in a cloud that made him cough and handed him the can.

"Are you trying to kill me?" he asked.

"Yes, definitely. That's how a real mastermind kills someone: with hairspray. And stop scratching your face. You'll mess up the makeup."

"But it's so itchy! How do girls deal with this all day?"

I laughed. "We don't wear several layers of the cheap stuff. Now stop it. I put a lot of work into those eyebrows. I don't want you messing them up."

He rolled his eyes. "Fine, fine. But I'm removing this the second the final bows are over."

"You can't. Little kids are going to want to take pictures with the handsome and funny Gaston."

He sighed an exceptionally dramatic sigh. "Fine. I'll suffer for my art. And my fans."

"How noble of you."

He bowed with flair, the exact bow he'd be doing on stage in a few minutes, and kissed my hand. Even that somewhat silly gesture was enough to make me flush.

Mr. King waved his arms to get our attention and stood center stage, just behind the curtain. "This is always my most treasured and most despised moment in the theater: the moment I have the honor of watching my truly incredible thespians perform to the best of their ability and profit off of their hard work, and the moment when I must begin the painful process of bidding farewell to this production and this particular cast. To my seniors, Drew, Wesley, Jorie, Sienna, Rafael, Elizabeth, Devon, Caroline, and Jackson: it has been a true delight to have worked with you all. To my leads, Rachel, Drew, Wesley, Sienna, and Rafael: thank you for bringing Belle, the Beast, Gaston, Mrs. Potts, and Lumiere to life. To my stage hands and stage director: thank you for all of the important work you do off stage.

"And finally, thank you Jorie and Wesley for having the gumption to step up and act when the fate of this production hung in the balance. We would not be here with you. A round of applause for everyone."

Everyone clapped, and I had that distinct feeling again, the one I'd had the day Mr. King told us the musical was a for sure thing. That feeling that I didn't want this moment to end, that I didn't want to say goodbye to the theater program at River Glen Academy. It was a conflicted feeling, a wonderful feeling confused by an immense sadness. I wondered if this was just a part of life. I'd always heard adults talk about high school in negative terms and how they would never go back if they had the option. I couldn't understand that reaction. I didn't want to leave.

"And now," Mr. King said with a flick of his wrists, "showtime!"

The music started playing, and when Rachel made eye contact with me across the stage where she waited for her cue, I motioned for her to take a deep breath. I performed my short part of standing with Elizabeth and Tiffany, gushing over Gaston's appeal, and headed off stage to watch the rest of the scene. Rachel was practically glowing. It seemed she was growing more confident with every note she nailed, and her performance was just getting better. I was truly wowed by her.

The moment that Wesley stepped on stage, the audience started laughing. I couldn't see his face from where I was standing off stage, but I'd seen this performance enough times in rehearsals to know that he had hilarious facial expressions, and with the exaggerated eyebrows I'd drawn on him, I was sure it was extra funny.

I wondered if he would still do theater in college. It might have been a little far from the community theater once he started UT, but maybe he would join UT's theater program or find a community theater in Tampa. I hoped he would. I loved watching him perform.

Watching him now strut across the stage in ridiculous fashion, propping his arm up on Jamar's head, and acting outraged at the sight of Belle reading, even though his performance was silly and fun, I caught myself smiling not because of the humor of the scene but because of Wesley. I'd told my mother in the middle of a hysterical fit that I thought I loved him, and though the words surprised even me when they came out, I hadn't given it any more thought after that. I hadn't known where we stood until prom, and even then, I was just so happy to have him. But now, watching him and thinking of everything we had shared over the years, I recognized that I did, in fact, love him, and I felt a kind of peaceful joy at that realization.

***

When the play was over, and everyone had taken their final bows, the cast stayed on stage to take pictures with their friends, family, and elementary students who wanted pictures. One of the cutest things about doing Disney musicals was that a lot of the elementary students got so sucked into the magic that they didn't realize it was a performance and not real. The main characters had to stay in character while talking to elementary students just like the day we saw Rachel and came up with the name Spotlight Heroes. She was at it again but with Drew by her side this time, and kids were literally lined up to take a picture with the princess and newly transformed prince. There were a few little girls also waiting for pictures with Wesley, and he was lifting them in the air and eliciting giggles all around. At one point, some underclassmen girls who definitely had a thing for him tried to convince him to take a picture with his arms around them, but he declared, in character, that he would not be seen with any woman except Belle and gave me a wink. It was such a good feeling knowing that that gesture and wink were really directed at me.

"Miss Haywood," Mr. King said as he walked up beside me, "Wonderful work with the sets tonight."

"Thanks, but I think we need to adjust the sets for the dining room tomorrow. Sarah can hardly see around that wardrobe costume, and she tripped and nearly fell during 'Be Our Guest.'"

"Noted. Now, Miss Haywood, I had a query I was hoping you could answer."

"What's that?"

"I know many of you seniors have already made your plans for next year, but I was wondering if this is the end of the road for Spotlight Heroes."

"Oh, well—"

"I don't want it to sound like I'm asking for money, of course. But Spotlight Heroes is such a wonderful creation. I'd hate to see this be the end of its hero journey."

"I actually hadn't decided. I was thinking of keeping it going, but I'm not sure yet."

"I hope you do. I know several wonderful peers who could benefit from something like this. And if I'm not the beneficiary, I'd love to be a member of your illustrious board."

"I'll definitely keep that in mind. I've enjoyed working on it so much that I don't know if I want to let it go."

"Wonderful news."

"Actually, I'm really sad that this whole thing is ending. It's been so much fun."

"To all things a season."

"It's too bad I can't just do high school musicals perpetually."

"No, but I wouldn't turn away an alum who wanted to volunteer to help with sets or performances. If you're in the area next year, you are always welcome on my stage."

"Thank you, Mr. King," I said. "I'll keep that in mind."

He walked away to talk to some parents, and I hung back on the stage a few moments. Coming back to River Glen to volunteer was a dream come true. I could keep Spotlight Heroes running and get to work with Mr. King again. This made the idea of graduating and leaving much easier to take.

But how could I do all that from Gainesville?

22

— · —

The din in the hotel ballroom was deafening. The sheer number of people who had chosen to enter this competition was intimidating to say the least, but I tried to remain confident in my project with Wesley. I was extremely grateful in this moment that I hadn't taken on this thing alone. Seeing Wesley's smile and feeling my hand in his made this a little less terrifying.

I didn't have a problem with public speaking; in fact, I'd always been pretty good at it. But the scale of this thing was enough to make anyone nervous regardless of inherent skill. I didn't think there were this many high schoolers in all of Polk County, let alone enough interested in a complex project. I wondered if other schools assigned this rather than making it extra credit like Ms. Corwin did.

Each project had an assigned location, so Wesley and I checked in, got our number, and headed off to find our assigned table. We had had our poster professionally printed because Wesley had insisted that it would look better than a tri-fold, and looking around now, I was glad we had. About half of the groups had professionally printed posters, and the ones who didn't definitely stood out. I wasn't sure if that would really make a difference if the ideas were good, but there was no doubt that first impressions mattered at an event like this.

At our assigned table of #45, Wesley got to work hanging the poster, and I set up our mini-posters of spreadsheets and pictures from the fundraisers and musical itself. I finished before Wesley, so I took a moment to glance around at the nearby posters that I could see to get a sense of the competition. The projects were varied. Some were arts, some STEM, some athletic, while others focused more on student activism or representation or even family-based projects. I was extremely intimidated by the caliber of some of the projects, and I could only see the ones immediately around me. I started to feel pretty anxious about competing against all of these other projects.

"Finally got it," Wesley said, standing back to admire the product of his exceptional poster hanging skills. "What do you think?"

I inhaled slowly, then exhaled. "Wesley, I don't know about this."

"You think I should move the poster?"

"No, I don't know about this." I gestured wildly around me. "All of these projects are really good."

"Not all of them. There's a guy over there with an alarm clock that sprays you with water. Like, who wants that? Plus, this isn't a middle school science fair, and—"

"Wesley."

He reached out his hands, and I gladly took them. "Are you okay? You look kind of pale."

"How are we supposed to even have a chance of winning when there are this many people here?"

He squeezed my hands. "Hey, we have a great project. It's unique, impactful, and interesting. We have a good chance. And besides, we don't need to win."

"Yes we do."

"We don't. We just need to be really impressive, and we've got that handled. It'll be fine."

"I'm really nervous."

He pulled me toward him and wrapped his arms around me. "You'll be great. It's a chill set up. People walk around, you tell them about your incredible idea, and they'll keep walking. It's no pressure."

"I'm really glad you're here."

"Me, too."

***

After an impressively boring speech from the director of the competition, the event kicked off, and judges, college admissions reps, parents, teachers, and local politicians started milling around the room. Wesley and I didn't see much action for the first half hour or so since we were toward the back of the room, but I was somewhat grateful for that. It gave me a chance to observe the process for a little while. Parents, teachers, and local politicians didn't hang around for long, but the judges seemed to loiter quite a bit. It was the college reps that were interesting: at some projects they stayed for as long as the judges, and for others, they barely stopped walking as they passed by. I got the sense that loitering from them was a good sign.

Ms. Corwin found us and gave us a hearty wave as she walked up. "I'm so glad to see you both."

"You, too, Ms. Corwin," I said.

"When you get a chance, you should swing by the left side of the room. Kendall has a very interesting STEM project over there, and Tiffany, Avery, and Hannah collaborated on a voting activism event."

"Oh yeah, I remember signing one of their petitions."

"Me, too," Wesley said.

"Well," Ms. Corwin said, "your project looks lovely, and I must say that the musical was a smash success. Mr. King hasn't been able to stop talking about the two of you at staff meetings. He's so glad that the musical happened, and he's very proud. I'm also very proud. I know you were reluctant in the beginning, but I'm very happy that you both decided to enter. If Spotlight Heroes continues, I am happy to remain on the board if you'd like."

"Definitely," I said without thinking, then risked a glance at Wesley, but he didn't seem phased.

"Well, I'm going to circulate a bit, but I'll be back later. By the way, I haven't seen that many dealing with arts, much less theater, so you might have something here."

"Thanks, Ms. Corwin," Wesley said.

After she walked away, I said, "Sorry about that."

"About what?"

"I didn't mean to imply that Spotlight Heroes was moving forward. I know you're on the fence about that."

"Jorie, Spotlight Heroes is your baby. If you want it to move forward, then do it."

"But you said—"

"I didn't want to add more to the project, and maybe I was a little harsh, but I know you want to keep this thing going. I can tell how enthusiastic you are about it."

A smile cracked on my face. "I am enthusiastic about it. I just don't know how to make it work."

"You'll figure it out."

"Jorie." I heard my name, but couldn't quite figure out where it was coming from. I turned around a few times before I connected the guy waving at me with Dr. Jameson from USF.

"Dr. Jameson. Sorry, I wasn't expecting to see you here."

"Well, I wasn't sure that I would be able to get away to see the project, but I managed to work it out. I hope you don't mind, but I brought Evelyn Yeats with me. Evelyn works in the dean's office. I thought she might be interested as well."

"Nice to meet you." I turned toward Wesley. "This is Wesley Dixon. He's my partner in the project. Wesley, this is Dr. Jameson. He's one of the poly sci professors that I met at USF."

"Glad you could make it," Wesley said as he shook his hand.

"Well," Dr. Jameson said, "I won't take up too much of your time, but I wanted to be sure I heard about your project. Do you mind if we hang around for a while and listen to your presentation?"

"Of course not, feel free."

Seemingly out of nowhere, the panel of judges popped up next to us inquiring about the project, and I couldn't help but wonder if Dr. Jameson had seen them coming and chosen this exact opportunity to make himself known.

Wesley and I presented the project exactly as we had rehearsed it, divvying up the parts of the project based on what we had done or what we understood best. He'd gotten pretty annoyed with me when I made him practice it with me repeatedly the night before, but now I was grateful that I had harassed him into it. I felt capable of reciting this presentation in my sleep, which helped tremendously with my nerves. The judges seemed pleasant enough, and they asked a lot of questions, though I wasn't sure if that was a good sign or a bad one. After the appropriate amount of time—it seemed to be about ten minutes per presentation—they moved on, and I exhaled fully for the first time in about as long. Dr. Jameson promised to circle back after taking a look around with Evelyn, and as soon as we were alone again, Wesley stole a quick kiss.

"Well, we did it," he said.

I nodded. "Now we wait."

"What are we going to do with the prize money?"

"A little ahead of yourself there, Dixon. We haven't won."

"Yet. We've got a great chance. So? Money?"

"I don't know. I had just always planned for you to take it for your car."

"Don't need that anymore."

"Maybe I'll just donate it to Spotlight Heroes."

"You've got to do something fun with at least part of it."

I rolled my eyes. "Like what?"

"I don't know, buy something stupid that you've always wanted."

"Hey, nothing I really want is stupid."

He raised an eyebrow. "Kinetic sand?"

I pointed a finger in his face. "That stuff is amazing, and you know it."

Just as I was scolding Wesley with a finger inches from his face, an older woman walked up to our table and began eyeing our poster. I glanced over to see who she was, and though I didn't know her, I couldn't have missed the UF logo on her shirt.

"Uh, hi, can I answer any questions for you?" I asked.

She smiled. "Yes, I'd love to hear about this."

She introduced herself, and I gave her the abbreviated version, and when she asked a few questions, I gave her more details. She seemed to be doing a job but also genuinely interested. I wonder if the interest was actually genuine or if she was just good at faking it for all these high school kids.

"This is a very intriguing project," she said, "and I must commend you on your ingenuity and ambition. Creating your own nonprofit is an idea I haven't seen before. It's very impressive to find young people who are as resourceful, creative, and determined as the two of you. That's why I love coming to contests like this."

"Thank you," I said. "That means a lot."

She handed each of us a card. "I'm afraid I have to leave before this event is officially over, but do send me an email letting me know the results regardless. I'd be interested to talk to you both some more."

"I'll do that. Thank you."

She left, and I screamed silently as Wesley hugged me, picking me up off the ground.

"That's huge, Jorie."

"I know"

"You definitely have to email her."

"If we win."

He shook his head. "Either way. That could be your chance."

"You could email her, too."

"What for? I got the school I wanted. Promise me you'll email her no matter what."

"I promise."

***

Dale Henchard was a large, somewhat intimidating man if you didn't know him. He towered over everyone, and his low, booming voice hardly needed a microphone, but everyone in town also knew that he was a big softy when it came to stuff like this. He was a super nice guy and just wanted to give back. But when he took the stage to announce the winner, the room was solemn and quiet.

"It has been an honor to see so many incredible projects. I look forward to coming years when the bright young minds in this room grow up and change the world for the better. But today, winners must be chosen. I am grateful to our panel of judges for making the hard decisions.

"Our first place winner of $1000 personally and $5000 to their cause is Group #56 Gerald Travolo and John Smith for their work on a sustainable community garden."

Wesley scoffed. "STEM always wins first place."

"What happened to 'we don't have to win'?" Wesley never cared about winning, but I couldn't ignore the pang of anxiety that struck my heart hearing that we hadn't won. Would second or third still be enough for UF? And what if we didn't place at all?

"I still stand by that."

"Second place of $500 personally and $3000 to their cause is Group #7 Whitney Arnell, who developed a tutoring program specifically for differently abled athletes. And our third prize of $300 personally and $2000 to their cause is Group #45 Marjorie Haywood and Wesley Dixon who created a nonprofit to save their school's musical production."

I was so sure that I wouldn't hear Dale Henchard say our names that when he did, I hardly heard them. They mostly washed over me without my realizing until Wesley's arms were around me, and the sound of his cheering shocked my senses. We had placed third. I hadn't thought this could happen. I had hoped we would win first place for weeks, but today, seeing all of the projects, I became convinced we had no chance. And now we had placed third. We had won $300. Spotlight Heroes was about to receive a two grand donation.

Spotlight Heroes had a chance of moving on.

***

That night, I composed two emails. The first was to Dr. Jameson. He had been there to see me and Wesley receive the third place prize, but he had asked that I send him an email with detailed reports of the project and the nonprofit so that he could forward the information to the department and the dean. He was very confident in my chances of earning a scholarship, and he had urged me once again to consider USF.

The second email was to the UF rep who had given me her card at the competition. I notified her of my status on the waitlist and asked that she forward the information to the admissions committee as well as anyone else she deemed worthy of knowing.

I didn't send either email right away. I opened both drafts side by side on my laptop. Dr. Jameson's email on the left was long. It included detailed descriptions, attachments of spreadsheets and documents and analyses. I thanked him profusely for his support and enthusiasm. The UF email included all of the same attachments, but it was shorter, void of the personal connection I had made with Dr. Jameson, void of the enthusiasm I had shared over the project with him.

I couldn't have explained if someone had asked, but the emails looked wrong next to each other. Shouldn't the UF email be longer, more effusive, more *something* than the USF one? Shouldn't all of the enthusiasm and excitement be in the UF email? And why was the prospect of pressing send on the USF email easier than the UF one?

I pushed the computer back a few inches and rested my head on my fist, staring at the emails. I didn't like the way I felt looking at the emails. I had entered a contest, lied to my best friend, and spent countless invaluable hours of senior year working on this project to get into UF, to convince them that putting me on the waitlist was a mistake. Here before me sat a typed email with a blinking cursor that could set all of that in motion. Yet, it seemed weird now to send the email.

I clicked send on the email to Dr. Jameson, keeping the UF one open. Had I let myself get distracted by my conversations with Dr. Jameson? Surely there were professors at UF who would be as supportive, and even if there weren't, that didn't mean I couldn't move forward with Spotlight Heroes anyway. Who said I needed a professor's help? I could do it on my own.

I pulled my computer to me again and clicked send on the UF email before I could think about it anymore. I closed my laptop, shoved it on my nightstand, turned off my bedside lamp, and lied down to sleep.

This is what I had wanted. UF was within reach.

So why did I feel so weird about it?

23

Wesley opened the passenger door of his car so I could get out. Taylor's house was kind of out in the middle of nowhere, and without any nearby streetlights, it was hard to see the ground. I wore cowboy boots in preparation of walking all over the mysterious ground, but I was still glad to let Wesley walk in front of me so that I could see if he suddenly fell into an ant hill or something.

"Don't forget the bag in the back," Wesley said, taking my hand and helping me stand.

I grabbed the bag. Even though Taylor had forbidden me from getting her a graduation gift—she said it was stupid since we were both graduating—I had found the perfect gift and couldn't resist.

I hadn't let go of Wesley's hand, and with the gift bag in my other hand, we walked toward the barn. Taylor's parents were cattle ranchers, so they had a pretty substantial amount of land. There was a barn close to the house that was used in the early ranching days, but as they expanded, they built a bigger barn and converted the old one into a cool party spot for Taylor and her siblings. It had a loft area with bunk beds for sleepovers, a huge blank wall onto which they would project movies, and a lounge area with big comfy sofas and mini fridges with sodas. Even though Taylor lived further away from River Glen than most of us, we usually had big parties at her house just because she had the barn. Plus, if her dad was in a good mood, he'd give us a hayride.

Tonight was Taylor's graduation party, and even though by this point in the year, I'd been to approximately a million graduation parties, I was most looking forward to Taylor's because she threw the best parties. Walking up to the barn, I could already hear the music blaring. It was a good thing the closest neighbors were several acres away.

I was about to turn the corner to the screen door of the barn when Wesley gently pulled back on my hand, spinning me around to face him.

"One sec," he said.

Before I could ask why, his hands moved into their familiar places on the sides of my neck, and he kissed me slowly but firmly. I wrapped my free arm around his waist and just enjoyed the moment. Even though it was night, it was still hot outside, and I could feel the heat radiating off of Wesley's back. He started to pull back, then, thinking better of it, leaned in for one more kiss before finally taking a step back.

"Just had to get that in," he said with a smile.

"No opposition here."

He held out his hand again for me to take. "Ready?"

I nodded, and we walked into the party hand in hand. The music was loud, and it looked like most people were dancing. Taylor immediately rushed over and hugged us both. When she saw the yellow gift bag in my hand, she frowned.

"I said no gifts."

I waved the bag in front of her face. "Well, I decided that I didn't care what you said."

Taylor rolled her eyes and tossed the tissue paper to the side. She pulled out the book—the illustrated version of *Jane Eyre*, which was her favorite book, with the art done by her favorite artist—and failed at suppressing the smile on her face.

"Where did you find this?"

"Where do you think? Amazon."

"But—but I said no gifts."

"Well, too bad. As your best friend, I know you too well, and I know that this is the perfect gift, and I'm giving it to you whether you like it or not."

"Fine." She clutched the book to her chest. "But I'm not keeping this for you. I'm keeping it for me."

"Whatever works for you."

Taylor practically skipped off to show her mom the book, and Wesley smirked when I made eye contact with him. He bowed in Gaston style and offered up his hand.

"Shall we dance?"

Laughter burst through my tightly closed lips. "We shall."

***

It was an incredible night. We danced, we sang along to music, we played card games, we swam in the pool for a little while, and we ended the night with Taylor's favorite: sparkling grape juice. The empty bottles were still floating in the pool. Drew joked that, from far away, it looked like a wild drinking party had just gone down.

Most of the people who weren't staying the night had left by then, and those who were staying hadn't quite gone in for the night even though it was closing in on midnight. Taylor's younger brother Aaron—a year younger than Savannah—had claimed the barn bunk beds, so it was decided that the boys would take the barn for the night and the girls would sleep in the house. Between Taylor's room and the guest room, there was plenty of space. Still, it seemed that no one was quite ready to move out of the barn party vibe even though just about everyone was clearly exhausted from all of the festivities. A few of us were collapsed on the couch, a few were playing video games upstairs in the loft, and some others were outside playing a game. Wesley and I were reclined on the couches. He tapped my arm with the hand around my shoulders and pointed at Drew, who was totally passed out asleep, sprawled out across the love seat. I had to swallow my laughter when I saw him.

"How long has he been like that?"

Wesley chuckled. "A while. He's out cold."

I glanced over at the other sofa. It was pretty far away from us. Caroline and Devon were over there, but Caroline had fallen asleep with her head in Devon's lap, and it looked like Devon was watching something on his phone.

"So," Wesley said, "graduation isn't that far away."

"Don't remind me."

"Not excited? Why?"

"I'm looking forward to college, don't get me wrong," I said. "I'm just not excited for all of this to end. I like high school. I like our friends. I like nights like this. I just don't want things to change."

"Change is a part of life."

"I hate when people say that. It might be true, but it doesn't make it any less painful."

"Yeah, I'm gonna miss this, too." He didn't say anything for a while, then added, "Have you heard from UF yet?"

I shook my head against his shoulder. "Crickets."

"I'm sure they get a lot of emails like that. Just takes time."

"I guess."

Wesley shifted a little so he could look at my face. "What is it?"

"I've always been so sure of UF, you know?"

Wesley chuckled. "Oh, I know."

"But what if it's the wrong decision? What if that's not where I'm supposed to be?"

"Why would you say that?"

"It just feels wrong. I like River Glen. Maybe I don't want to leave it. At least not now. I hadn't put much thought into it before, but maybe I don't want to be that far away from home, from family, from friends. From you."

"Yeah, but if UF is the school for you, then—"

"But what if it isn't? I mean, there's all these cool opportunities if I stay. I could keep working on Spotlight Heroes."

"You could do that in Gainesville."

"Not without the board of directors. And what about Mr. King's offer? I couldn't do that from hours away. USF is less than an hour. And Dr. Jameson."

"There are good professors everywhere."

I sighed. "I guess so. I just wonder sometimes if I'm making the right decision. You've always been so sure of UT."

"You've always been so sure of UF."

"Yeah, but now I'm not sure, and you still are. What do you think?"

"I'm not going to tell you."

I sat up and faced him. "Why not?"

"Because I think you need to be the one to make that kind of decision. You shouldn't let me influence it."

"Please tell me? I care what you think."

Wesley closed his eyes, sighed, then opened them again. "Obviously, if I'm being totally selfish, I'd love for you to stay in the area. Heck, I'd talk you into UT if I could. I don't love the idea of being hours away from you, but I also don't want to be the thing that stands in the way of you doing everything you want to do. If you end up at UF, we'll make it work. Pick what makes you happy."

I settled back in against him, and he wrapped his arm around me again. Randomly, I would get this feeling that things were too perfect, too right. It seemed so surprising that Wesley and I had finally made it here to this place where we were together and happy without all of the confusion we'd had between us until now. I wasn't sure if this was the right time to say it, but I felt like I couldn't let the moment pass without saying it.

"Wesley?"

"Hmm?"

I tilted my head to look up at him. "I love you." He raised an eyebrow, and I saw the corners of his mouth start to lift upward. "I hope that doesn't freak you out or anything, but I just felt like I had to say it."

The smile finally broke free. "I love you, too, Jorie. I think I always have."

I wrapped my arm around his waist and let him kiss the top of my head.

This moment was perfect, just as our kiss on the dance floor at prom was perfect, just as our kiss on the Ferris wheel was perfect, just as standing off stage during the musical was perfect. These were the moments that I wanted to last forever. I decided that, in whatever way I could, I would find a way to make these moments last wherever I ended up next year.

***

The sun streamed in through the window, and I realized that Taylor forgot to close the curtains before she fell asleep last night. I stumbled out of the bed and yanked the curtain across the glass. There ended up being a lot more guys who stayed the night than girls, so Taylor, Caroline, and I were the only ones in Taylor's room with three more girls in the guest room. Wesley had texted me late last night to tell me that the loft in the barn was packed. He claimed that it was kind of awkward.

"What are you doing?" Taylor croaked out, rolling over in bed to face me.

"Closing the window. You forgot to close it. Again."

She chuckled softly. "Sorry. Hey, your phone is buzzing."

She tossed it to me, and I somehow managed to catch her errant throw. Wesley was texting me. It was still kind of early, so I doubted that the rest of the guys were awake. It was probably just Wesley.

Good morning, love.

I snickered at the text. *You're going to wear that word out now, aren't you?*

Absolutely.

My cheeks hurt from smiling as I tapped out a response. Suddenly, I got hit on the shoulder by a small stuffed turtle.

"Hey, what?"

Taylor said, "Is that Wesley?"

"Why would you say that?"

"Because you're bright red and smiling like the Joker."

"I do not smile like the Joker."

"Only when you think about Wesley."

"Oh, that's attractive."

"So is it him?" she asked, and I nodded. "Y'all are cute together. I'm glad you figured it out."

I was only half listening to Taylor because I was waiting for the next text from Wesley, but I decided to check my email while I waited. Taylor's house had terrible reception since it was so isolated, so it took a minute to load, but when it did, I saw an email from UF admissions.

Part of me was inexplicably tempted to turn off my phone and pretend that email didn't exist for a while. If it was bad news, I wasn't sure I wanted to read it right now, and I couldn't risk that it would be good news; not after what happened last time.

But could I ignore it?

"What now?" Taylor said. "That's definitely not a Wesley face, unless he said something creepy or something."

"It's an email from UF."

Taylor bolted upright. "Then open it."

Caroline rolled over in her sleeping bag, but she seemed to be asleep still. I shushed Taylor and sat on the edge of the bed where Taylor immediately hopped over to see over my shoulder.

"What if it's bad news?"

"What bad news? You're not in now. If you're still not in, nothing's changed."

"You know it's not that simple."

"What are you going to do, never open the email? Just do it."

I took a deep breath and clicked the email to open it. I tried to skim the email, but I wasn't comprehending any words, and I kept misreading things, so I forced myself to slow down. I could only hope that Taylor wasn't reading ahead and would react before I could comprehend anything.

Dear Miss Haywood,

Thank you for your continued enthusiasm for the University of Florida.

I stopped reading. The rule for college decisions letters was simple: "Congratulations" meant you were in, and "Thank you" meant you weren't. Did the same rules apply for waitlist emails to the admissions department? No one ever told you what to do when you were waitlisted.

We greatly appreciate being kept in the loop of your continued education. Spotlight Heroes sounds like an impressive endeavor, and we congratulate you on winning third place in the Crossroads of Education and Government competition. That is quite an accomplishment.

Come on, get to it. The longer this email became, the more convinced I became that I wasn't in.

In light of this information, your commitment to UF, and incoming admissions decisions, we would like to amend your admissions status from the waiting list to accepted.

It was as if Taylor was reading at the exact pace I was because she threw her arms around me and squealed as much as she could without waking Caroline.

"You did it," she said, squeezing another hug. "You got in."

"Yeah."

"What is it? Aren't you excited?"

"Yeah, of course I am, I just—I don't know. I thought I would be more excited than I am."

And that was true, at least. Why wasn't I more excited? UF had been my plan for years, and I was so sure of it. When it shifted from a sure thing and stopped being a guarantee, I had done everything imaginable to make it a reality. Now here it was, and I was happy to read the email, but it didn't feel like I thought it would. It didn't feel the same.

"So, what does that mean?" Taylor asked. "Are you not going to go to UF?"

"No," I said, but I wasn't sure I believed it. "Of course I'll go. This is what I've been planning. I just—"

"You don't want to leave Wesley?"

"No, I mean yes, I mean—it's not just Wesley. It's a lot of things. I don't know, I guess a lot has changed in these last few months. It just feels different."

"So what are you going to do?"

I flopped back on Taylor's bed. "I don't know."

***

School was nearly over, and everyone was in a flurry of preparations for final exams. My AP exams were already over, and, luckily, I was able to exempt two of my remaining exams. It felt weird going to classes and hearing the teachers wish us well in college, talk about graduation, and ask us to visit River Glen next year. I didn't know how to end a school year at River Glen without knowing I'd be back in two months. Every little thing felt so final, like a sense of loss.

I went to see Ms. Corwin to have her sign my exam exemption form. Hers was the last signature I needed, so I used my study hall to track her down. Luckily, it was her free period, too, so I wasn't interrupting a class.

"Ms. Corwin," I said as I walked in, "do you have a minute to sign my exemption form?"

"Of course, come on in," she said, waving her arm to gesture me in.

She took the form, signed it without even reading it, and looked up at me with a smile.

"So, how are you feeling about graduation?"

I chuckled. "Honestly? Terrible."

"Why is that?"

"I don't think I really want to leave high school."

"I don't hear many high school seniors say that."

"I know, it's weird."

"Don't feel bad for enjoying high school or having a good experience. You should be glad to have liked it. It's a wonderful thing that not many people get."

"I want to go to college, but I don't know if I'm ready to leave just yet."

"Have you decided on a college?"

I shook my head. "I thought I had, but now I'm not sure."

She gestured for me to sit down. "Walk me through your thought process."

"I always thought I'd go to UF. Always. For as long as I can remember, I've felt like UF was the right school. I thought I'd go to UF, then go to UF Law, and become a nonprofit lawyer."

"Why is that?"

I shrugged. I wasn't even sure myself. I remembered loving UF when I first saw it, but why? What had stood out to me? Why was I so confident that UF was the right school for me and that nothing else could compare? I was unsettled by the fact that I genuinely didn't know the answer to any of those questions.

Maybe I thought people would be impressed by my attending UF. Maybe I thought UF was just far enough away from home but not too far. Maybe I had just assumed that UF was better than other state schools simply because others did. I just didn't know anymore.

Except that maybe I *did* know. Maybe I did think all of those things in the past, but it was rapidly becoming clear to me that I just didn't feel that way anymore.

"I don't even know. I was just always set on it." And I really didn't know. It seemed hard now to quantify why I was so sure about UF. I certainly didn't feel that certainty now. In fact, more and more, I was feeling like what I wanted just wasn't going to be accomplished in Gainesville.

"Did something change that?"

I couldn't help but laugh. "Well, I didn't get in."

"Really? But I thought—"

"I didn't want anyone to know. I actually got waitlisted. I thought I could get off the waitlist and no one would ever know. Including you."

She smiled knowingly. "Ah. So that's why the change of heart for Crossroads of Education and Government."

I nodded. "I figured if I could do something impressive enough, UF would change their minds."

"And you and Wesley won third place. I'm very proud."

"Really?" I asked, and she nodded. "Thank you."

"And did it?"

"What?"

"Did it change their minds?" she asked, and I nodded. "So why the indecision now?"

I explained everything that had happened at USF, all about Dr. Jameson and the scholarship and Lana and Spotlight Heroes and everything else. I laid out every detail, and whether or not she really wanted all of that information, she listened intently. When I finally felt like I had explained everything, I sat back in my chair, and she smiled.

"You know, there's nothing wrong with changing your mind. USF is a great school, too."

Is that what I was doing? Was I changing my mind?

"I know, but I don't know if I really have changed my mind. I've been so sure about UF for so long. How do I know I wouldn't be making a mistake changing it now?"

She thought for a while before answering. "College is so much more than just the school you pick. It's the experience, the friends, the professors, the programs, the location, the cost, and everything else going on in your life aside from the classes themselves. All of that matters when picking a school."

"It just doesn't seem like an easy decision either way."

"It probably isn't. Picking a college usually isn't. But at the end of the day, you're the one who will spend four years there learning, living, and having fun. It needs to be the right decision for you no matter what other people think. Let me ask you this: do you want to continue Spotlight Heroes? Do you hope to do this during college and beyond?"

I nodded. "I think so, yeah."

"If you hadn't gotten into UF, would you have felt like Spotlight Heroes was a waste of time?"

"No."

"If you hadn't gotten into UF and the musical had still fallen through, would Spotlight Heroes have been a waste of time?"

I thought carefully. "No."

"Then regardless of what you choose, it sounds like Spotlight Heroes is something really important in your life that you want to continue. It fits in well with your plans for the future. So pick the school that fits into those plans, whatever those may be."

I fidgeted a little. "Will you tell me what you think I should do?"

She smiled but shook her head. "That's what Wesley said."

"He's a good friend."

I groaned. "I just wish it were easy."

"Important decisions rarely are. Choose what feels right for you. I believe you can accomplish your future goals at either school, but you need to choose what's right for you. Deep down, if you put aside everything and everyone else, ask yourself if there is a school that you're leaning toward."

The bell rang, so I thanked Ms. Corwin and left her room. I think I knew which way I was leaning.

24

High school graduation was one of those events that you watch in movies, you heard about from older people, maybe you even attended for your friends, but when it was you, it didn't feel real. I bought my graduation dress—royal blue like River Glen's colors, knee length and boat neck—months ago, but I didn't wear it until today. It felt weird putting it on now, like some kind of official ceremony was taking place. I straightened my hair and did my makeup, but none of it felt real. I wondered if everyone felt this way on their graduation day

"Yo," Savannah said as she flung my bedroom door open. "Wesley's here."

"Thanks."

"You're not even going to yell at me for coming in without knocking?"

I shook my head. "Not today."

"Oh no, don't tell me you're going to get all mushy on me."

"Am I not allowed to be sentimental on the day of my high school graduation?"

"Well, Mom's already crying, so try to keep it together, would you?"

She left, and I finished my mascara. I hadn't been able to decide on black heels or nude heels all week, so I closed my eyes and picked one. When I opened my eyes and saw the black shoes, I dropped them and put on the nude ones. It seemed that was the way with me now: picking one thing made me realize that what I really wanted was the other.

I walked downstairs and, predictably, found Wesley in the kitchen sneaking one of Mom's cupcakes.

"It's, like, nine in the morning," I said, and he jumped. "Little early for a cupcake, don't you think?"

"They're strawberry," he said with a mouthful of cupcake. "It's basically a scone."

"I don't think that's how that works."

"Well, it's working for me."

I laughed and handed him a napkin. "You're going to get pink frosting on your white shirt, and then your mom will kill me."

"Fat chance. She loves you. She'll kill me instead."

I tried not to notice too much how good Wesley looked. He was wearing a white shirt with navy pants and a navy vest. It was formal but unique, and that suited him really well. He wiped the pink icing from the side of his face and held out his hand, which I gladly took in mine.

"You look beautiful."

"Thank you," I said, then kissed him. "So what are you doing here? I thought we were meeting up at the school."

"We were, but I decided that I wanted to give you your gift now."

He held out a poorly wrapped square gift with an exceptionally tied bow. Clearly his mom had tried to compensate for his lack of wrapping abilities. I unwrapped the gift to find a boxed desk set including a yearly planner, a legal notepad, and a set of really pretty pens. The entire set was blue, and it was pretty without being frilly. I looked up at Wesley, and he smiled.

"For Spotlight Heroes, so that you can continue to plan stuff. And the planner's for college: whichever one that is."

"I love it."

"Good."

"And speaking of college, I have news for you."

His eyes brightened. "You finally picked one?"

"Finally?"

"You know what I mean. So which one won out?"

In response, I grabbed my phone and pulled up the email I had sent to the admissions department notifying them of my acceptance. I handed my phone to Wesley who took it eagerly, and when he saw the notable section, he lifted his eyes and smiled just slightly.

"USF?" he asked.

I nodded. "USF."

"Jorie," he said before kissing me and giving me a powerful hug. "I'm so happy for you."

"Thank you."

He rubbed the back of his neck. "And, selfishly, I'm glad we'll both be in Tampa."

"Definitely a major pro for USF."

He chuckled nervously. "Uh, not that I'm not excited, but what on earth happened to UF?"

I shrugged and smiled. "It wasn't the right school. I had convinced myself that it was, but I never really looked into how I would fit there. USF has so many things that I want."

And it was all true. I had a weird obsession with UF based on nothing, really. It was all based on some warped belief I had that good students at Florida high schools can only go to UF. I'd put UF on this weird pedestal for absolutely no reason. I never considered whether what UF had to offer is what I wanted—I just kind of assumed that it was. There was nothing wrong with UF, and I still liked so many things about it, but I hadn't obsessed over UF for reasons that would actually benefit me as a student. All I cared about was my degree saying "The University of Florida," and in the end, USF made it possible for me to do everything I wanted all at once. I never gave USF the time of day, and though I'd never admit it to my mother, if we hadn't visited USF that day, I may have never figured it out at all. It came down to the fact that I had never given USF a chance.

I was learning to give more chances. Giving USF a chance had worked out. Giving Wesley a chance to understand me and forgive me was the best thing I could have done. Giving my parents a chance to be a part of my decision-making had only helped me. Being stubborn and stuck in my ways had only caused me and those around me pain. As it turned out, I much preferred giving out some chances.

"Does your family know yet?"

I nodded. "My mom has already ordered, like, five USF shirts for each of us."

He laughed. "Of course."

"And remember that girl Lana that I told you about? The one I met at the USF meet and greet? We're going to coordinate so that we can be roommates."

"Nice."

"Can you believe it? I can't imagine telling my past self that I would pick USF, or really any other school, over UF."

Wesley took each of my hands in his. "Things change."

"They certainly do."

It seemed surreal and yet totally normal at the same time to be at this place. I was going to USF, I was dating my best friend, I was the founder of a nonprofit organization, and I was thoroughly happy about all of those things. I couldn't have guessed a few years ago, or even a few months ago, that this would be how my life would look on the day of my high school graduation. But I was really looking forward to the future—the real future, not the imagined future I made up in my head. The real future was so much better.

"So, are you ready?"

I thought for a moment. "To graduate? Jury's still out. To go to college? Absolutely."

In a few hours, we would graduate high school, and the rest of our lives would begin. I was still a little hesitant and afraid to leave River Glen Academy, but I was confident in who I was now. I always thought my life would begin with one word: congratulations. It didn't even begin with "Thank you for applying." It began long before that, though I hadn't recognized it until now. It began with me.

EPILOGUE

Along with everyone else, I stood to applaud the talented cast of the River Glen community theater. Many had thought Gian was being too ambitious picking *The Sound of Music*, but he had pulled it off beautifully. It had definitely been a case of timing. Rachel, of course, sang the part of Maria perfectly, and opposite Wesley as Captain von Trapp, the performance sparkled. I wasn't usually a big fan of children singing, but the kids playing the von Trapp children were really good.

The standing ovation lasted for several minutes, and as it went on, I admired the costumes everyone was wearing. Some of them had been borrowed from River Glen Academy, some from nearby Jackson School for the Performing Arts, and others were donated by the local consignment shop. It hadn't been easy finding matching children's outfits that looked like they were made from curtains, but I'd managed to pull it off.

The sets were really good, too. They had mostly been built by the cast, though the money for the supplies had been fronted by a fundraiser at Evan's. Gian had drawn a beautiful field for the opening scene, but the hardest sets were the von Trapp household sets. They were so intricate, and they had to be painted on so many different boards to allow the actors to enter from multiple places as they would in a really big house like that.

The applause died down, the cast took their final bows, and I rushed out of my seat to meet Wesley at the front. He had already attracted a crowd of people praising his performance, but when he saw me, he smiled and held out his hand through the crowd for me to reach him. Once I was close enough, he slipped an arm around my waist, and Rachel gave me a big hug.

"Thanks for coming," she said. "What did you think?"

"Oh my goodness, it was incredible," I said. "You guys nailed it."

"Thank you."

Wesley sighed with a smile. "This was definitely the hardest role I've ever done. Gaston was a lot easier."

I laughed. "Well, both were really good."

Gian spotted me and waved as he came over to us. "Jorie, so glad you could make it."

"Of course. Thanks for the prime seat."

He spread his arms. "Had to reserve a seat for our special benefactor. We couldn't have done it without you."

"I don't think I technically count as a benefactor. I didn't donate money."

"You might as well have. You organized so many events. This production wouldn't have looked nearly as good without the help of Spotlight Heroes."

I was so glad I had chosen to stay nearby in Tampa. Spotlight Heroes had been able to help River Glen and other schools and community theaters. I never could have done this if I had gone to UF. I would have been too far away.

I smiled. "I'm just happy I could help. Keep me in mind for the fall musical. I'll only be less than an hour away."

"Oh, I definitely will."

Gian walked away, and Wesley furrowed his eyebrows at me. "Aren't you helping Mr. King in the fall with the play?"

I shrugged. "Can't I do both?"

He laughed and rolled his eyes. "You're a workaholic, you know that?"

"And proud of it."

"So am I." He kissed me on the cheek, and several people in the crowd made jokes about Captain von Trapp cheating on Maria.

"Ready to start school?"

"Don't remind me. I feel like I've been so busy with *The Sound of Music* all summer pretty much since we graduated. Two weeks before starting school doesn't seem like enough."

"Hey, count yourself lucky," Rachel said. "River Glen goes back on Monday."

He laughed. "Fair enough. What about you, Jorie?"

"I'm definitely ready to start. By the way, once we move in, Lana wants to have dinner."

"Definitely."

"Did you ever pick a major?"

Wesley laughed. "Communications."

"Seems pretty broad and unspecific."

"Exactly. But I'm minoring in theater. I hear the fall musical will be *Fiddler on the Roof*. Think I'm up for it?"

"Definitely."

"It's going to be weird being a part of a musical without you. I mean, even the community theater ones, if you weren't in them, you still helped out."

I laughed. "I don't think the University of Tampa needs the help of Spotlight Heroes."

He laughed, too. "Maybe not. But I hear there's a commun ty theater in Tampa that's been struggling."

"Sounds like a perfect opportunity. You're still on the board, right?"

"You'll have to kick me off if you want me gone."

This time, I kissed his cheek. "That won't be necessary. By the way, I think I will double major in business. This thing is taking off, and it couldn't hurt, right?"

He smirked. "Workaholic."

I took his hand and pulled him off the side, away from the crowds, and kissed him for real. It was a little jarring because I could smell the cheap foundation on his face, but I felt his lips curling into a smile, and that made me smile, too. It was so nice knowing that, in two weeks when we went off to college, we would be less than half an hour from each other.

It was equally as nice knowing that I could come back to River Glen whenever I wanted I understood why some people wanted to move away for school, but more and more, I was realizing that I definitely didn't want that. I thought I did, but after everything that happened, I was thrilled to be staying close. If someone had told me six months ago that I would discover that USF was the perfect school, I would have laughed in their face, and, in fact, I had thought my mother was crazy for even suggesting it. But now, I was excited to be starting USF in two weeks.

After all, I still had law school to look forward to at UF.

* * *

ACKNOWLEDGEMENTS

A hearty thanks to everyone who supported the writing of this book over many years. I am very grateful for the family members and friends who encouraged me along the way. Thank you to Kayla Tirrell and Morgan Brownlee for being tireless readers of my work always. I can't even tell you how much it is appreciated. Thank you to friends who always supported my ambitions even when I didn't know how to support them myself: Makaylee Graves, Kristen Christensen, Laina Strickland, Kelly Layne, Jill Jones, Carly Faller, Katie Carroll, Emma Zimmerman, and so many more. Thank you to Trinitee Davis, Lyndsay Greene, Skyler Grooms, Grace Pagliaro, Grace Rodda, and Della Kate Terry for being such a wonderful focus group and test audience. I so appreciate your input and involvement.

Thank you to the University of South Florida for being the place where I wrote my first novel, where I first found a writing community, and where I realized I could actually write books. I knew when I wrote Jorie's story that USF would play a big role in it as it has in my own story.

Thank you to Emerson College for being the second phase of my journey of learning how to be a writer. A special thanks to Jessica Treadway for being my thesis director when this story was nothing but something I had cranked out during NaNoWriMo. I'm so grateful for all that you contributed to this work and the ways you supported it always. Thank you also to Sara Novic for serving on my thesis committee and being a very early reader.

Thank you to NaNoWriMo for inspiring countless people to write a book. *Thank You for Applying* was first written as a NaNoWriMo project, and I'm so grateful that it gave me the push to finish this book.

Thank you to Lyssa at Booked Forever Shop for designing the cover of my dreams. You exceeded my expectations.

Thank you to Lakeland Christian School for being a place where I felt safe and loved. The teachers and friends I had there never wavered in their efforts to encourage me, and I can never begin to express my gratitude to everyone there. I wanted my high school experience to make it into a book because it was so meaningful to me.

Thank you to my students. It is a joy and a privilege to teach you all every day, and I'm so grateful to be in your lives. I hope this a book you want to take off the shelf and read. I hope it feels like a story for you because it is.

Thank you to the teachers who encouraged a love of reading and writing that already existed but needed a push: Rebeka Corgan, Judy Oncu, and Tricia Latham. You taught me that books could be magical and that I was capable of creating that magic. I am a teacher now because of teachers like you.

Thank you to my sister for being someone who dreams big and never lets anyone get in the way. Thank you to my parents Brian and Sylvia for being my most consistent and passionate supporters and letting me read books that were far beyond my ability level as a child. I wouldn't be here without you.

ABOUT THE AUTHOR

When she's not writing about high school students, she's teaching them AP and DE English. Kristen Grafton is a Florida native with an MFA in Popular Fiction & Publishing and an MA in English Rhetoric. She was a triple major in college. She has an unhealthy obsession with her cats and Taylor Swift.

To learn more about Kristen Grafton, follow her on Twitter/X @KristenMGrafton, Instagram @kmgrafton1, and visit www.kristen mgrafton.com.

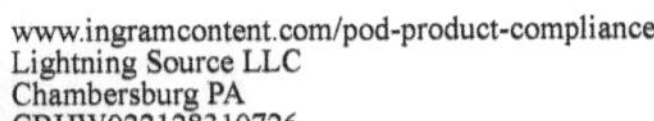
9 798218 407377